Ravel

A Listener's Guide

Victor Lederer

AMADEUS
PRESS
An Imprint of Hal Leonard Corporation

Published in 2015 by Amadeus Press
An Imprint of Hal Leonard Corporation
7777 West Bluemound Road
Milwaukee, WI 53213

Trade Book Division Editorial Offices
33 Plymouth St., Montclair, NJ 07042

Printed in the United States of America

Book design by Snow Creative Services

Library of Congress Cataloging-in-Publication Data

Lederer, Victor.
Ravel : a listener's guide / Victor Lederer.
pages cm — (Unlocking the Masters series ; 27)
Includes bibliographical references.
ISBN 978-1-57467-477-4
1. Ravel, Maurice, 1875–1937—Criticism and interpretation. I. Title.
ML410.R23L43 2015
780.92—dc23
2015030423

www.amadeuspress.com

To the memory of Joe Dougherty

Contents

Acknowledgments

Thanks to the usual crew: Elaine, Karen, Paul, and Kate. Thanks as always to my editor, Bob Levine. Thanks again to my sharp-eyed copy editor, Iris Bass. Particular thanks are due to Bernie Rose for his help with beautiful samplings from the piano works and elucidation of Ravel's harmonic methods.

Understanding Ravel

There's no question that the beautiful surfaces of Maurice Ravel's music provide an easy approach, but subterranean strengths are what make it last. So, in one sense, his works hardly seems to need analysis, partially explaining their immense popularity, while the tug of the composer's sophisticated compositional technique—his tart harmonies and rhythmic playfulness, for example—and his singular way of expressing passion keeps it from superficiality, bringing one back to listen, again and again.

Ravel's style, gorgeous on the outside but steely underneath, derives its irresistible outward beauty chiefly from long-spun melodies as well as some of the most skillful and effective instrumental and vocal writing by any composer in any era. His structural strength comes from rhythmic freedom, harmonic richness, and daring, and formal patterns that are mostly straightforward but well suited to the job. Ravel's gifts as a composer also include the related qualities of brevity, concision, and momentum: he says what he has to say and keeps moving, never dragging his material out. Much of the master's oeuvre is in dance form, most famously perhaps his various essays in the waltz, but he also composed in *Daphnis et Chloé* one of the great ballets. But in several other cases that we'll see, he also transcribed or otherwise reworked his music into ballets: he seemed to be thinking constantly in terms of its choreographic possibilities. More difficult to explain but present just the same is his ability to evoke passion at a distance, a peculiar skill at which he may be unmatched.

Ravel's typically builds his melodies out of short phrases that he repeats and enlarges, giving them a sense of an unfolding, organic growth. Two notable examples are the supple melody from *Ondine*, the first movement of the piano suite *Gaspard de la nuit*; a second is the famous one describing sunrise that opens the third part of *Daphnis et Chloé*. In both cases, Ravel's method makes the listener feel as though present at their birth. Whether for piano alone, chamber ensemble, or full symphony orchestra, his instrumental writing is remarkable above all for its transparency, the sense that even in the most densely written passages every note can be heard. Ravel admired Mozart, whose instrumental textures display a similar lightness and clarity, and his own contemporary Richard Strauss, whose heavily scored orchestral works are also remarkably lucid. Mozart, of course, worked with smaller forces, but all three masters stand among music's greatest orchestrators.

The high level of Ravel's technique helped him in the writing of brilliant and idiomatic music for voice in his fifty-nine songs, many of which stand among the most beautiful and approachable in the hermetic world of the art song. The master approached each lyric with almost complete freedom and openness in his treatments. His accompaniments are also unusually varied, with some as is normal for piano, others for chamber ensembles, and still others for large symphony orchestras. *Idiomatic* may be the last word to describe his two operas, though, as both fly in the face of operatic convention. The second of the two, *L'Enfant et les sortilèges*—"The Child and the Spells"—has achieved moderate popularity. But the first, *L'Heure espagnole*—"The Spanish Hour"—remains, despite its technical polish and other qualities, a harder sell.

Probing beneath the lovely surfaces of his style, Ravel's rhythmic freedom is notable, lending his music a rare fluidity. He changes metrical patterns often, usually to follow the flow of a melody, and with such ease that it's rarely noticeable. He's also (along with Brahms) the master of a rhythmic device with the alarming name hemiola. This is simply the placement of two-note phrases into a three-beat pulse, like that of a waltz, but it gives the effect of a slight irregularity, a sort of hiccup in the rhythm. What sets Ravel apart are his wit in contriving them and skill at weaving them into the musical fabric.

To us, in a context of later, more aggressively dissonant music, Ravel's sounds comfortable and easy to grasp. But he actually uses dissonance very freely, and was considered radical early in his career. This is music in which the harmonic underpinning is carefully sculpted to avoid the expected direction or resolution. You'll hear this technique used with particular skill in the *Valses nobles et sentimentales*. Ravel favored open chords with a floating sound over the regular, solid ones that usually end tonal compositions. He also liked the sound of two mild dissonances (sevenths and ninths) in particular, both of which soften the edges of his harmony, giving a bronzed quality that's part of his characteristic sound. As a highly educated and trained musician, Ravel additionally knew and employed archaic harmonic patterns when he wanted to evoke antiquity.

His countryman and fellow impressionist master Debussy rigorously avoided many traditional forms: you'll be hard pressed to find contrapuntal writing (the horizontal, note-against-note technique that's rarely absent from the work of Bach) or sonata-type developments (the pitting of theme against theme, as in Haydn or Beethoven) in his work. Both Debussy and Ravel had been trained at the Paris Conservatoire, France's top music school, and both knew musical structures like these inside and out. Less dogmatic than Debussy, Ravel used such techniques sparingly, and with a light hand when he did: the *Sonatine* and the fugal second movement of *Le Tombeau de Couperin* display his formal skills, but with notable delicacy in both cases. More typical for Ravel is the simple, three-part (ABA) pattern, where the two outer sections are alike or nearly so, and the middle of a contrasting nature, be it of tempo, key, rhythm, texture, or some combination of these elements. Well employed, this three-part pattern can carry considerable expressive weight, with the return of the opening section potentially quite momentous. Dance forms, such as waltzes and minuets, are almost invariably in three-part form; since Ravel wrote so much music in dance forms, it was completely natural for him to turn to it often.

Dance forms are pervasive in Ravel's oeuvre, but most are abstract and at an ironic remove from actual dancing. In this respect he follows the pattern of composers he admired: Chopin, whose waltzes and mazurkas are meditations on dance rather than real dances, or Schumann, the dance movements of whose early piano works are fantastical, ironic, and laden with echoes. Ravel considered many of his instrumental works for conversion into ballet, but even *Daphnis et Chloé*, his grandest score, is hardly ever danced now, perhaps because the music is too interesting on its own.

All these qualities add up to a style that's as distinctive as it is beautiful. What sets Ravel apart, however, is a singular gift at evoking dammed-up emotion. As with Debussy, a layer of irony forms part of Ravel's style: neither composer wears his heart on his sleeve. Instead, a reticent, carefully cultivated coolness of manner, reinforced by some of the most impeccably tailored surfaces in music, contain Ravel's passions, and the resulting tension is irresistibly poignant. Moments that display it abound. You'll have no trouble in hearing the high emotion surging just below the surface but held in check, especially in places where melodic phrases reach upward but the volume drops, the composer's dusty harmonic language doing its part to soften edges. The resulting sense is of a longing that's intimate but sharp, rendered unsentimentally. When Ravel reaches ecstasy, his catharses are all the more telling for breaking through the pervading restraint.

Ravel was active in a period when the related influences of nationalism, exoticism, and orientalism in music were high, and the context of all three affected the composer's ear and pen in the most profound ways. Nationalism found its way into European music in the 1830s, as Chopin's Polish masterpieces—chiefly the mazurkas and polonaises—broke molds, exciting listeners and performers alike with their irresistible beauty and power. Chopin was soon followed by Liszt, who paraded his Hungarian origins in a variety of music, mostly the *Hungarian Rhapsodies* that are actually influenced by Gypsy music. But later Bartók and Kodály picked up the Hungarian cause, studying and gaining inspiration from the stranger, less flamboyant real folk music of their country. There's a Russian school, including good and great composers, such as Glinka, Mussorgsky, Balakirev, and Rimsky-Korsakov; Dvořák, Smetana, and Janáček formed a brilliant Czech wing; Sibelius represented Finland, and Grieg, Norway. The depth of the impact of this movement on mainstream European music is impossible to overestimate. Suddenly the exciting rhythms, mournful melodic patterns, and pungent harmonies of Gypsy music could even be heard in the conservative formalist Brahms; his *Hungarian Dances* are marvelous individual expressions of nationalist color, and the thrilling finale of his Piano Quartet in G Minor (Op. 25 No.1) is a Gypsy romp set at the end of a serious chamber work. For a good seventy-five years from the middle of the nineteenth century, "classical" European music was saturated in the colors of folk song and dance.

The regional music of Spain stands apart as a special case. Poorer and more set in its traditional ways than the modern, industrialized societies of England, France, Germany and postunification Italy, Spain had in Falla, Albeniz, and Granados excellent native composers to write in the Spanish manner. But French musicians from the last quarter of the nineteenth century and the first quarter of the twentieth were also drawn to the music of Spain for its eroticism, moodiness, and rhythmic snap. The list of French composers who composed brilliantly in a Spanish idiom is long and impressive, and Ravel is right at the top. Perhaps his love for Spain came through his mother, a Basque from the border region of southwestern France, but it may be that his formidable skill at evoking Spain in music was nothing more or less than that of a gifted musical mimic working in a popular idiom of his time. Certainly his Spanish pieces are as high in Iberian color and scent as those by his countrymen Bizet, Chabrier, and Debussy.

What attracted French composers to the music of Spain was perhaps above all the wailing, North African sound of its flamenco-based melodic material: Ravel even described the melody of his *Boléro* as "folk tunes of the usual Spanish-Arabian kind." But, like other composers of the age, Ravel welcomed just about any exotic influence. Rimsky-Korsakov looked away from Russia to write a *Capriccio espagnol*, as did Tchaikovsky for his *Capriccio italien*. A look over a list of Ravel's compositions shows an astonishingly wide range of influences, including Basque, Greek, Hebrew, Yiddish, Scottish, and French folk music, as well as Viennese waltz. His skill with archaic melodic and harmonic patterns allowed him to evoke antiquity in the same way; and although his source for the lyrics of the *Chansons madécasses* turned out to be fraudulent, Ravel's sensuous evocation of a hot Madagascan setting is persuasive.

Last among Ravel's exotic influences are those of Middle and Far Eastern music, a benign by-product of European colonialism, now known as orientalism. As identified and described in 1978 by the American academic Edward Said, orientalism can be summarized as the tendency by Europeans and Americans to simplify and reduce the lives, beliefs, and arts of colonized nations' peoples into formulas. Said's studies dealt primarily with economic and political domination of England and France over North Africa and the Middle East in the nineteenth and early twentieth centuries. Questions and objections to aspects of Said's theory have been raised, but the broad points of his arguments are by now widely accepted.

Orientalism spilled over into European literature, fine arts, home decor, and music, peaking right around 1900, just as Ravel came into his maturity. He, Debussy, and others came into contact with unfamiliar music by Russian composers as well as the utterly foreign sounds of Javanese orchestras at the 1889 Paris Exposition. Loving what they heard for its novelty and freshness, French composers changed direction, blending impressions of non-Western instruments, intervals, and rhythms into their works. These would-be Asian sounds are what identify orientalist music; this should be nothing more than a new label for tinkling or wailing musical mannerisms you're already familiar with. Verdi's *Aida*, completed in 1871 to celebrate the opening of the Cairo Opera House, is one of the earliest and greatest works showing orientalist influence. To give an idea of its sway, works as familiar but different in mood and purpose as *Aida*, Sullivan's *The Mikado* of 1885, and Mahler's *Das Lied von der Erde* of 1909 are displays of musical orientalism; and European and American music from about 1870 to 1925 contains countless examples.

The quasi-Asiatic sounds in these works now echo with varying degrees of success, with some now coming across as tired and tasteless. (One might cite the "Bacchanal" from Saint-Saëns's otherwise admirable opera *Samson et Dalila* as an example.) Ravel's restraint keeps his music within the bounds of good taste for most listeners. The most orientalist of his works are the song cycle *Shéhérazade* of 1903, a movement from *Ma Mère l'Oye*—"Mother Goose"—of 1911, and a scene in *L'Enfant et les sortilèges*, his second opera, completed in 1925. In that work offense is piled on top of offense as a China cup and a black teapot engage in a duet consisting of alternating lines of mock-Asian and mock–African American gibberish, a racist joke in Colette's libretto set by Ravel to music that's brilliant and charming. You just have to remember that it was acceptable at the time. Other works, perhaps most notably the String Quartet and the Piano Trio, also show Asian musical seasoning in less concentrated forms. While exotic and orientalist influences abound in Ravel, his rapid pacing and the purifying filter of his style keeps them fresh. Always searching for new sounds and ideas, later in his career he blended influences of jazz and blues he'd heard.

While open to any interesting stimulus, Ravel was a proudly French musician, whose influences, as you might expect, included the eighteenth-century masters Couperin and Rameau, his teacher Fauré, Massenet, and Bizet, as well as the lively and charming music of Emmanuel Chabrier. Mozart seemed to him a divine figure, whose productivity he envied but tragically could not achieve himself. However, Ravel studied Mozart's style from the beginning to the end of his career. Although later Ravel was honored by the establishment that had attacked him when young, he never stopped supporting and encouraging the new and the radical in music. Among nineteenth-century composers he revered Chopin, whose perfectionism stood as a model, and with whom those who love both composers can readily find kinship. Although less of a perfectionist, Liszt was also an obvious and salutary source of inspiration and study for Ravel, who admired and learned from Liszt's harmonic boldness and advanced ideas about pianistic and orchestral sonorities. The music of the Russian school, particularly that of Mussorgsky, had an enormous impact on Ravel, as it did on Debussy, as well. The profound effect of the minimally trained but prodigiously gifted Mussorgsky on the Conservatoire-taught Frenchmen is worth considering. Familiarity should not dim the boldness and originality of Mussorgsky's *Pictures at an Exhibition*, where quasi-visual impressions drive the music. Its effect on Ravel and Debussy is obvious, and Ravel would transcribe the work for orchestra in 1922.

Often lumped together under the impressionist banner, Ravel and Debussy are remarkable for similarities in their careers, but they differed in many ways, too. Certainly these near contemporaries carried the modernist banner in France, and the pictorial inspirations that stimulated both do make for some interesting point-by-point comparisons. Both composers were bitten by the Spanish bug, and both wrote great works for the piano and for orchestra in the Spanish idiom; also, both conceived great music that evokes the water. Each wrote one beautiful, seminal string quartet. Although Ravel was fearless, Debussy was nevertheless the bolder harmonist. Ravel, however, was more inventive in his instrumental writing. As noted earlier, Debussy bent over backward to avoid formalism; Ravel used forms, but carried them effortlessly. The two initially had a cordial relationship, but their supporters and the press drove them apart. As you'll see, until Debussy's death in 1918, the two masters worked on similar ideas throughout their careers, evidently goading and spurring each other on in rivalry and matched tributes to the others' latest accomplishment.

Like Chopin's, Ravel's style was set early, mutating and flowering into somewhat more advanced manners over the course of his career. His relatively small output is typically divided into three periods: the early period, up about to the *Miroirs* for piano from 1905; the middle phase, until the outbreak of World War

I in 1914; and the late period, everything up to the end of his ability to work, in 1933. (An unidentified neurological malady silenced Ravel from then until his death in 1937.) In general, the early-period works show their origin in the late romantic era, and of course more influence of his teachers and the musical idols he imitated. The middle period shows him in full command of a rich and opulent style that's fluent, smooth, and strong; and the third displays leaner, drier, more open textures as the works of his friend Stravinsky and others made their mark. As is fairly typical for composers, all three of Ravel's stylistic periods contain music that looks ahead as well as back, so it's probably best not to lean too heavily on these rather arbitrary divisions.

Although he may have digested the advances made by other musicians, Ravel's style always remains clearly and unquestionably his own. Even though you may be able to point at an influence here or there, his integration of them is so complete that there's never a sense that he's mimicking or copying—unless, as in a couple of rather minor instances, he wants you to. Finally, within this small output is an unusually high percentage of the composer's works transcribed from one form to another. There are several reasons for this, and we'll examine these, as well as the music itself, in chapter 4.

I discovered while working on the book that generalizing about Ravel's music is unwise. For instance, several late-period works are rich and heavily scored, going completely against the prevailing leaner manner. And, while I tend to prefer the piano versions of many works (usually the originals) to the orchestral transcriptions that the composer made later, I found that with *Ma Mère l'Oye*, I love both the four-hand piano original and the orchestrated version equally. Everything Ravel published was crafted with the utmost care, and you need to hear every note and to keep an open mind.

2 His Life

Joseph Maurice Ravel was born on March 7, 1875, in Ciboure, a flyspeck on the map that's actually a suburb of Saint-Jean-de-Luz, a fishing town and resort in the southwestern corner of France, a few miles from the Spanish border. Ravel's mother, born Marie Delouart, was of Basque origin, explaining the presence of the Ravel family in this remote corner of France. Then as now, the Basque region was divided between France and Spain. Ravel identified strongly with his Basque origins, visiting his mother's native region many times even after her death, writing notes in the impenetrable language, and enjoying pelota, the national sport that's similar to handball and squash.

The composer's Swiss-born father, Pierre Joseph Ravel, was an engineer and industrial designer whose interest in mechanics the composer inherited. Three years later a second son, Edouard, was born in Paris, where the family had moved a few months after the birth of Maurice. Bright and well educated in the French secular manner, Maurice Ravel showed an early interest in and aptitude for music. He took lessons in composition, harmony, and counterpoint, and studied the piano, which he played fluently though not really well enough to make a career of performing his own works for the instrument—all of which are challenging—in public. As Ravel got older, his willingness to practice for its own sake decreased, and more skilled players had to be drafted to perform his piano music in public. A major formative event in Ravel's musical life was the International Exposition of 1889 in Paris, where Asian music, notably that of Javanese gamelan orchestras, was performed, opening many ears and changing the way musicians heard. Music by Russian composers, then relatively unfamiliar in Paris, was also performed, and similarly made a profound impact, steering French and other composers into heavy experimentation with a new range of sounds and harmonies, moving their interests beyond the nationalistic and merely exotic and toward the orientalist. The 1889 Exposition seems to mark the start of the high age of orientalism in European music.

In France, professional careers, including those of musicians, begin and run along tracks that include education at institutions at which students are prepared carefully and specifically for their future jobs. In 1889, Ravel was admitted by examination to the Paris Conservatoire, the leading music school in France. But his time at the Conservatoire was marked by an ever-growing incidence of failure to pass its mandatory competitions and blind, strict, often arbitrary examinations. Ravel's disappointment and disillusionment with the institution grew, and eventually he drifted away from the school, working on his own. The public popularity of the composer's music led many to question the authority of the Conservatoire, rupturing its faculty into camps and allowing rival groups, one of which Ravel joined, to promote the music of more modern-minded composers than what the Conservatoire typically turned out; although ironically, the revolutionary Debussy was not only a product of the Conservatoire, but a prize-winning one. That master simply went his own way after completing the Conservatoire program.

More formal rules govern musical composition than you might imagine, and when taught academically, these can oppress the imagination, as they did Ravel's. Good composers typically learn the rules prevalent in their age, then adapt, ignore, and flout them freely, with listeners sensing a boldness or freedom without necessarily understanding what's going on technically. (Of course, no one can argue that structure and discipline are bad in and of themselves.) In the mid-1890s, Ravel began writing his own works, including the *Menuet antique* for piano and a habanera that eventually found its way into the *Rapsodie espagnole* (see pages 90–95). Several *mélodies*—songs—also date to this earliest period. While hardly daring by his later standards, they were considered bold in their day and that environment, but were generally well received. In 1898, he began to study composition with Gabriel Fauré. A great composer himself, Fauré initially found Ravel's works difficult, but eventually came around to become a wholehearted supporter and friend.

Fauré brought Ravel into a *salon*—a informal, private group that would meet occasionally, in the home of a socially prominent host—where he met Debussy and other leading cultural figures, so even when young, Ravel traveled in high artistic circles, thereby gaining the glory of association with and implied approval of these groups. Meanwhile, conservative critics had begun to attack him, and before he turned twenty-five, he had become a symbol of the new, fresh, and exciting in French music. While in his twenties, Ravel also associated with contemporaries across the spectrum of the arts, in another informal, progressive-minded group that called itself the "Apaches." Two of the poets in the group, Léon-Paul Fargue and Léon Leclère, would supply the composer with lyrics he would set as songs. Others Apaches included the pianist Ricardo Viñes, who introduced many of the keyboard works of Debussy, Ravel, and others, and the fine Spanish composer Manuel de Falla.

Almost thirteen years older than Ravel, Claude Debussy was the dominant figure in French music at the turn of the twentieth century. The two composers had a cordial relationship until the press and supporters began to posit them as rivals. Debussy's more suspicious nature was piqued, and he pulled away from Ravel, who never saw himself as a competitor. As a student, for example, Ravel had ardently supported Debussy's then controversial opera *Pelléas et Mélisande*. But, while the two admired each other's work, their admiration was never granted without critical reservation on both sides. On at least two occasions, Ravel took pains to point out that he had accomplished certain stylistic landmarks earlier than Debussy, or that he perceived weaknesses in the orchestration of Debussy's symphonic work *La Mer*.[1] For his part, Debussy harshly criticized Ravel's song cycle *Histoires naturelles*. There is, however, a fascinating note from March 1904 in which Debussy offers concrete advice to Ravel regarding the dynamics—the loudness and softness—of his String Quartet in F Major, which the senior composer had heard in a rehearsal.[2] Six years younger than Ravel, Igor Stravinsky was the other major composer who was Ravel's colleague and friend. The Russian-born giant's career really took off once he began composing for the Ballets Russes in Paris.

The Prix de Rome was the highest award given out annually by the Conservatoire. Every year, students were subjected to three rounds of compositional trials, starting with a fugue and culminating in a large-scale cantata, all of which were judged blind. (Debussy had won the award in 1884.) Any infraction of the rules of composition, including the most obscure, were noted, and the jury, made up of distinguished teachers and composers, voted first, second, and third prize winners. Ravel dutifully made his submissions every year from 1900 to 1905, with the exception of 1904. The only award Ravel won during the five years he competed was to place third in 1901. Over these years, perhaps defiantly, he made technical errors that he probably knew would offend the jury. In the meantime, he had begun to strike out on his own, and in his own voice, with early masterworks in various forms. These included the song cycles *Shéhérazade* of 1903 and *Cinq Mélodies populaires grecques*, composed between 1904 and 1906; two extraordinary chamber works, the String Quartet of 1903, and the Introduction and Allegro for Harp, Flute, Clarinet, and String Quartet of 1905; and, finally, several crucial works for keyboard: *Jeux d'eau* of 1901, and the *Sonatine* and *Miroirs*, both completed in 1905. It's hard to imagine our musical universe without these great works, and clearly a major career was on its way, no matter how the Conservatoire jurists voted.

Ravel's rejection by the Conservatoire had turned into a public scandal, in which supporters who were not necessarily personal friends pointed out the absurdity of the juries' decisions and the flaws in their makeup as well as the pointlessness of the competition if a talent like Ravel's could not win. After the 1903 contest, Fauré accused the jury of cooking the result, and *l'affaire Ravel*—the Ravel question, or scandal—peaked in 1905. The publicity only helped Ravel, turning the Conservatoire into a symbol of hidebound institutionalism, absurdly insistent that to be good music had to follow its rules, deaf to the qualities of an imagination like his because he had violated a few of them. The ultimate irony is the obvious sophistication of Ravel's techniques.

Life as a professional composer arrived for Ravel in stages between 1902 and 1905, as his split with the Conservatoire became permanent. He began an intensely productive cycle of roughly ten years, brought to an end by the onset of World War I. Works of this, his high middle period, make up a roll call of masterworks in all categories. Piano music begins with the *Sonatine*, fine-boned but passionate, followed by *Miroirs*—"Mirrors"—a suite of independent tone poems, much like Debussy's *Estampes*—"Prints"—of 1901 or his two sets of *Images*, the first of which was also published in 1905. (This was a golden age of piano music in France.) Three years later Ravel composed *Gaspard de la nuit*, the landmark for keyboard with a title that's difficult to translate (see pages 37–43). One of the summits of the composer's achievement as well as of the piano literature, the three movements of *Gaspard* are separate but unified spiritually as well as by their difficulty, that of the third part being legendary. The *Valses nobles et sentimentales* of 1911, based on the waltz suites of others (notably Schubert, Chopin, and Schumann) but subjected to hauntingly dissonant harmony and fragmentation, forms another crucial work, not only for the piano, but in twentieth-century music. A crossover from piano to orchestra is the great ballet *Ma Mère l'Oye*—"Mother Goose"—which occupied the composer between 1908 and 1910. In the realm of chamber music, there was, at the beginning of the period, the Introduction and Allegro for Harp, Flute, Clarinet, and String Quartet, with the great Trio for Piano, Violin, and Cello in A Minor of 1914 rounding it out. As with many composers, Ravel's vocal music is not as well known as his other categories, but he composed many works for voice in this decade, including the song cycles *Histoires naturelles* and *Chants populaires*. The musically advanced *Trois Poèmes de Stéphane Mallarmé* date from the end of this phase. Ravel completed *L'Heure espagnole*, the first of his two operas, in 1909. Finally, two of his important orchestral works, the *Rapsodie espagnole* of 1908, and his grandest canvas, *Daphnis et Chloé*, completed in 1912, also come from this period.

To the outside world, the process of writing music is in equal parts mysterious and sacred. Music seems to gush from some, such as Bach, Haydn, and Mozart; whereas Beethoven's struggles to shape recalcitrant material are legendary. (In fact, all of them had to sit at a desk or keyboard and plug methodically away.) Ravel seems to have fallen somewhere between these extremes of musical legend, looking on composition as a *métier*, what the French respectfully call a craft, while also sensing a higher purpose to his work. But during the writing of *Gaspard*, Ravel began to struggle more and more with creating material, and his output dropped drastically after World War I.[3] He also began to devote more time to recasting his own work and that of others in transcriptions, usually from piano to orchestra, but sometimes going in the other direction; in any case, easier work than inventing new music. As we'll see, the taxi accident in which the composer was injured in 1932 seems to have closed the door on his already troubled creativity. However, as noted in the previous chapter, it's unwise to generalize about Ravel's work. His two piano concertos are among his last works, but they teem with ideas, and the *Concerto pour la main gauche*—Concerto for the Left Hand—is scored with great richness, even a deliberate heaviness.

Ravel's father died in September 1908. Little has been said of the composer's personal life because he kept his nonprofessional activities private; few facts emerged after his death. For example, he often went out for long nocturnal outings, but no one knows where he went or what he did. He was close to both parents, particularly his mother, and to his brother. His father's death hit him hard, and his mother's, in 1917, would devastate him. Ravel never married, and there's considerable speculation about his sexual orientation; Benjamin Ivry's sympathetic biography *Maurice Ravel: A Life* is based on the premise that the composer was a closeted gay man in a supremely intolerant age. While certainly possible, there's no proof either way, and, as every biographer likes to point out, Ravel's closest relationship was clearly the one with his mother.

Diminutive but wiry and exceptionally handsome, Ravel dressed as a dandy when young, becoming more restrained but with a continued taste for startling elements, such as brightly colored socks and suspenders, as he matured. As an adolescent, he affected an ironic manner, which he seems never to have quite given up. A coolness or awkwardness on the composer's part are often mentioned in biographical accounts; the warm-hearted pianist Arthur Rubinstein spoke of his "complete indifference for everybody around him,"[4] but Ravel was, as noted, close to his family and to an inner circle to which Rubinstein evidently did not belong.

Nevertheless, Ravel seems to have been a reliable friend to that inner circle and an honest, spite-free judge of musical merit. He was fearless in defending his own music against performers' distortions in the name of interpretation, including even a dragon like Arturo Toscanini, whom he argued with publicly after the conductor led a performance of the *Boléro* at too quick a tempo. Ravel had many disputes with performers, including the pianist Ricardo Viñes, an old and close friend to whom he entrusted the first performances of many of his keyboard works until Viñes over-interpreted and Ravel lost faith in him; the composer's battles with the one-armed pianist Paul Wittgenstein over the *Concerto pour la main gauche* are well documented. Yet the impression one gets of Ravel the man is somehow positive: perhaps less crazy than many composers, he comes across as a hard-working professional who knew his own worth and what he wanted, but who could relax and participate comfortably in some social settings. We do know that he was secular and irreligious and leaned to the left politically, and that he liked food and drink, and smoked heavily.

The guarantee of Ravel's renown surely was his commission in 1909 from the Ballets Russes, for what would become his orchestral masterwork *Daphnis et Chloé*. Three difficult years in the making, this great composition was accompanied by the kind of turmoil typical of productions under the dance company's brilliant, erratic director, Sergei Diaghilev. Only rarely with money in hand, Diaghilev managed to persuade composers, including Debussy, Stravinsky (for some of his most important ballets), and

Richard Strauss, to create scores from fine to immortal for his Ballets Russes. *Daphnis* was Ravel's only contribution, though as we'll see, he tried a couple of times more to work with the exasperating Diaghilev.

Ravel and Debussy were France's most famous composers when World War I broke out in August 1914. The war changed Ravel's life and musical style, then at its grandest and most opulent. Like Debussy, he was a fierce patriot, helping to care for wounded soldiers as they began to trickle back to Basque country where he was working as early as September 1914. Ravel volunteered for the French Army, but was initially turned down, apparently because he was too short and underweight. At the same time, he began work on his great piano suite, *Le Tombeau de Couperin*, a tribute to French musical heroes; he would ultimately dedicate each of the work's six movements to the memory of a fallen friend or acquaintance. In March 1915, Ravel reapplied for service and was accepted for duty as a truck driver and mechanic, but it was not until about a year later that he was sent to serve near the front line at the catastrophic Battle of Verdun.

Ill with dysentery, Ravel was returned in September to Paris to convalesce. But on January 5, 1917, his mother died. Although she was seventy-six and failing, Marie Delouart Ravel's death was an enormous blow to the composer. A month later, he was returned to the front, where his shaky emotional state led to his own decline, and to another furlough that put him back in Paris; through 1917 and 1918, he worked on a variety of musical projects, including *Tombeau* and the editing of a complete edition of the piano works of Mendelssohn. Ravel's health remained poor through 1918, his grief almost certainly playing a role. With the end of the war in November 1918, he was free to resume his life and work, shadowed though it was by sorrow and illness, both of which gradually passed.

A state of war also existed between the French musical establishment, more or less represented by the Société Nationale de Musique, which had been founded in 1871 to support French musical values in the wake of the Franco-Prussian War, and the radical elements in French music. Unorganized until the founding of the Société Musicale Indépendante (SMI) in 1909, this group represented more progressive composers' ideas, including (of course) those of Ravel. Formed chiefly by students and supporters of Fauré, the SMI would sponsor the premieres of many of Ravel's works from 1910 on. His bad experiences with competitions at the Conservatoire and his success once he decided to strike out on his own put him easily and solidly in the camp of the more radical composers, which also included Debussy, Satie, and Stravinsky. It may be hard for us to imagine that Ravel's music pushed the limits of musical expression when first performed one hundred years ago. Having the benefit and cushion of time to digest his edgy dissonances and formal experiments, the music now falls well within our aural comfort zones; but it emphatically did not to conservatives on juries and in audiences when new. For example, in a 1928 essay, the astute English musicologist Donald Francis Tovey cites Ravel as an example of "composers with atonal styles."[5] I hope as you read and listen that you'll be reminded of Ravel's radicalism, particularly in harmony, his formal daring, and of the sheer strangeness that marks much of his output.

Nineteen-twenty saw the composition of *La Valse*, a shattering farewell to imperial Europe. Ravel composed this landmark score, compact but powerful, for the Ballets Russes. Perhaps not entirely off base, Diaghilev commented, "But it's not a ballet, it's a portrait of a ballet."[6] Ravel silently picked up the score and walked out, another large hole opened in his relationship with the impresario. In an unambiguous sign of the wide esteem Ravel had achieved, however, the French government nominated him for the Légion d'honneur—"the Legion of Honor"—its highest award. Embittered by his youthful experiences with establishment organizations, and stating that he was antipathetic to worldly honors, Ravel declined the award. Yet Ravel readily accepted honors from foreign governments and organizations, because he felt that these imposed no endorsement of their policies; he didn't want to be obligated in that way to the French government.[7]

Nineteen-twenty was also the year Ravel began to compose *L'Enfant et les sortilèges*, his second opera, to a libretto by the revered writer Colette. He also began working in a more pared-down style that would characterize many, though not all, of his late works. The Sonata for Violin and Cello, begun in 1920 and completed two years later, is a linear, intellectual composition very much in his late manner. Debussy had died in 1918, and Ravel was now, unofficially at least, regarded as France's most important composer. He found himself the darling of the establishment and, ironically, the object of criticism by a younger generation of French composers, spurred on by his former friend, now sworn enemy Erik Satie.

Ravel spent the next several years working, in his now painfully slow way, on new compositions, and on transcriptions of his own work as well as that of others, including Mussorgsky's *Pictures at an Exhibition*, transforming it from its awkward but sincere original form for piano into a glittering orchestral vehicle. He also toured Europe, attending performances and occasionally conducting, though his style of leading an orchestra, like that of his piano playing, was clearly unimpressive and the object of criticism. The mid-1920s saw the creation of the *Tzigane*, as well as the *Chansons madécasses*; work intensified on *L'Enfant et les sortilèges*, which had its premiere in Monte Carlo in March 1925. The Sonata for

Violin and Piano, very much in the composer's condensed, often bare "late" manner, was completed, after four years of work, and introduced in 1927.

A triumphal tour of the United States, with a couple of side trips to Canada, occupied Ravel for the first four months of 1928. The composer's fame had, in the age of radio and easier transatlantic travel, extended readily to America and he was feted from the moment he arrived in New York. He slept better on trains than he did in his own bed, and behaved politely, even apparently, with a shy charm. And he was treated everywhere with a respect far exceeding what he received in France. Ravel visited many cities, including Boston, Detroit, Chicago, San Francisco, and Phoenix, where a side trip to the Grand Canyon left him staggered. He met George Gershwin, whose classical ambitions he encouraged, suggesting study with his colleague Nadia Boulanger, which never occurred. He loved to go to jazz clubs, the influence of which can clearly be heard in at least several of the few works he completed before his death nine years later. The engineer's son sought out tours of factories, including the Ford auto plant near Detroit. In the fall of 1928, Ravel accepted an honorary degree from Oxford University. In this year so busy with touring and other shows of respect, he completed only one work, the *Boléro.* He did, however, begin the two concertos for piano that stand among his greatest achievements.

Ravel spent the next two years touring Europe to attend festivals, conducting occasionally, and to work, in his now sporadic and tormented way, on the piano concertos. He wrote and talked about projects, including an opera-oratorio, but nothing came of these. Ravel's creative apparatus had begun, inexplicably, to freeze up, even though his final works—the song cycle *Don Quichotte à Dulcinée* and the concertos—are all great, with affects from charming in the case of the songs to heaven storming for that of the *Concerto pour la main gauche.* The latter and the Piano Concerto in G Major received their premieres in January 1932; although different in character, both concertos, his most important late works, are, paradoxically, rich in ideas.

On October 8 of that year, while riding in a taxi in Paris, Ravel was injured in a serious collision, taking cuts to his head, face, and chest. He walked to a clinic for treatment, but was badly shaken. Several months passed before he could resume his normal pace; his long decline, mental and physical, began within months after the accident. Some friends thought him to be increasingly withdrawn even several years before, and certainly his growing difficulty in writing music suggest a problem of some kind, whether psychological or organic. While no firm conclusion about illness can be drawn from his life before the taxi accident of 1932, his decline afterward is obvious, even if the illness can't be identified to the letter. Ravel, once sharp of mind and tongue, gradually grew gray and vague: physicians were unable to help, and prescribed long rests. In 1935 he managed a trip to Spain and North Africa with a friend, but spent months of his last few years visiting clinics in France and Switzerland, hoping for an improvement that never came. Yet his symptoms were peculiarly inconsistent. For example, he coached a pianist learning the *Concerto pour la main gauche*, certainly a complex task, yet he couldn't compose or play the piano himself. Ravel attended concerts, supposedly commenting intelligently on the performances. He lamented, "I still have so much music in my head."[8] Neurologists disagreed on the cause, and X-rays revealed no tumor. Finally a neurosurgeon attempted surgery to inject serum. The procedure failed, and Ravel died on December 28, 1937. There appears to have been no autopsy, and as is often the case in France, medical records were not made public. The neurologist, writer, and music lover Oliver Sacks speculates that the cause was Pick's disease, a type of aphasia in which the patient loses the ability to deal with abstract concepts or symbols, such as musical notation:[9] a terrible silence to be imposed on so eloquent a mind. Right after Ravel's death, one musician offered the composer's friend Manuel Rosenthal some rough-edged consolation, mixed with respect for the high level of his oeuvre: "At least he's not leaving any rubbish behind."[10]

3

The Piano Music

Indeed, Ravel left no rubbish behind; he was, without question, one of the great self-critics and editors in music. Anything he published had to meet stringent standards, and his entire oeuvre is, like Chopin's, of high and even quality. But in some essential way, Ravel's compositions for piano occupy a central place in his output. As we've seen, when young he played skillfully, at least until he gave up practicing, and he composed at the instrument, the arena and locus of his musical imagination. Some of his most familiar orchestral works are transcriptions of piano pieces that we'll examine in this chapter, while others, perhaps most obviously *Jeux d'eau* and *Gaspard de la nuit*, are by and for the instrument, difficult to imagine in any other packaging. Almost the entire catalog is of high significance, although some works—notably the complete *Le Tombeau de Couperin*—are performed infrequently and consequently are not enjoyed and appreciated as widely as they might be.

Ravel's works for solo piano span his earliest years as a composer to his high maturity, but do not come from his final period, roughly from 1920 on. (The concertos are for piano and orchestra.) *Le Tombeau de Couperin*, his neo-baroque suite completed in 1917, points toward the leaner style of the final period, while speaking eloquently in its own idiom. The early *Pavane pour une infante défunte* may be the master's most popular work, but the

Jeux d'eau of 1901 is greater and more important in Ravel's development, as well as in the history of piano music. The *Sonatine*, *Miroirs*, and *Gaspard de la nuit* are lush, passionate products of his high middle period, although the transparency of the *Sonatine* predicts his later style. With the four-hand piano version of *Ma Mère l'Oye* and the *Valses nobles et sentimentales* we see him moving toward lighter textures, of which *Tombeau* is the logical outcome.

Menuet antique

Ravel composed this earliest of his piano works in the repertory in 1895. He copies in tone and straightforward format the *Menuet pompeux*—"Pompous Minuet" (and yes, that's its title)—by the underrated French composer Emmanuel Chabrier (1841–1894). Both follow the ABA format used since the mid-eighteenth century, where outer sections flank a middle part of contrasting character. Ravel knew the Chabrier piece well, orchestrating it brilliantly in 1919 for the Ballets Russes. Chabrier's minuet is really entertaining, with a big personality. That composer set the outer parts in a rattling, almost comically aggressive manner that Ravel copies but scales back, and Chabrier's central section is more ripe and sweet than Ravel's. The youthful *Menuet* offers little competition with the masterworks of Ravel's maturity, but it's a charming work, even impressive in its way.

A proud phrase in an irregular gait opens the *Menuet*, accompanied by a mild dissonance that's an early example of a Ravelian stylistic fingerprint. Following Chabrier's procedure, and anticipating the tone of the songs *Épigrammes de Clément Marot*, Ravel ends this big-boned phrase on a deliberately archaic harmony. The middle section contrasts with the opening in all ways: where the outer sections are stern, this is gentle, soft against their loud, and sweet in the change of key from minor to major. Ravel casts its melody in a fluent rhythm more characteristic of the minuet than the unusual broken phrases of the outer sections. He also transforms a thunderous left-hand octave phrase from the "A" section into gently rising chords in the right. The closing section repeats the opening literally.

Pavane pour une infante défunte

Far more familiar than the *Menuet antique* is this evocative and gorgeous morsel from 1899, which may be Ravel's most famous work. As with the *Menuet*, he would travel far beyond the *Pavane*, yet the piece represents him well. The title means "Pavane for a dead princess": a pavane is a slow and stately dance that coalesced in the Renaissance; the dead princess is Ravel's fanciful embroidery to what would otherwise be a cool, rather spare title for the work. *Infanta* was the official title for the princesses of the Spanish royal family, thus giving a Spanish twist to the title of the *pavane*, if not the music.

While formally more elaborate than the *Menuet antique*, the *Pavane* is still easy to hear. Broad in tempo, but not too slow—Ravel supposedly remarked that the princess is dead, not the pavane itself—the piece opens directly with the noble melody that has kept it famous, over a weaving accompaniment provided by both hands. Its phrasing is subtle and unusual, expanding in second and third sections of the tune. An emphatic comment thickly scored in the middle of the keyboard and below rounds out its presentation. In Ravel's typical manner, the second melody expresses passion as from an immense distance, here suggesting that of time. Set over pulsing accompaniment, this penetrating tune is placed higher on the keyboard than is the opening melody. The second tune receives another iteration over a slow-moving accompaniment, and Ravel closes with a phrase in characteristically dusty harmony. The opening idea is then repeated, over arpeggiated chords in the left hand that suggest the strumming of a lute.

The central panel of the *Pavane* opens high on the keyboard but is soon and repeatedly pulled down with figures that sound like closing phrases. After several attempts this third tune manages to rise, and the effect is moving. But again, we feel what we're hearing is as from a distance, with Ravel's hazy harmonies crucial to the sense of remoteness. The opening melody is brought back for a single, eloquent statement, over arpeggios and a rippling figure, and the cadential phrases finally bring the *Pavane* to an end. The open, incomplete-sounding harmony of the final chords suggests ancient music and antiquity itself, once more. The ability to evoke a cloudy past with a blend of freshness and passion is a gift Ravel shows here and in works of his maturity, notably *Le Tombeau de Couperin*.

Jeux d'eau

Ravel composed this groundbreaking work (CD Track 1) in 1901. The title, which means "Fountains," intentionally invites comparison with a late (1877) work by Liszt, the *Jeux d'eaux à la Villa d'Este*—"Fountains at the Villa d'Este." Although Ravel copies Liszt's idea of using the keyboard to depict water, the two pieces differ in scale and character, with Liszt's being longer and meditatively lyrical, whereas Ravel's is lighter in texture and fantastical. An earlier piece by Liszt, *Au Bord d'une source*—"On the Bank of a Spring"—is in some ways a clearer ancestor, being purely sensuous and closer in proportion to Ravel's taut masterpiece. Although he admired Liszt, Ravel, in a work like *Jeux d'eau*, also displays Chopin's elegance and editorial severity: there are many notes in *Jeux d'eau*, but not one too many. Ravel gets credit for being an "impressionist" composer thanks to *Jeux d'eau*, where the aural mimesis of merging light and water is wonderful, even uncanny. Debussy composed several great piano works that also evoke water, perhaps most notably *Reflets dans l'eau*—"Reflections in the Water"—the opening piece of his first set of *Images*, written in 1905. Often accused of following and copying Debussy, Ravel pointed out that he had redefined pianistic images of water earlier; and for his part, Debussy repeatedly expressed his admiration for *Jeux d'eau*.

The work is a milestone for Ravel because it opens the way for the five impressionist tone poems that make up *Miroirs*, into which set *Jeux d'eau* could fit, even though Ravel reportedly wished he could put *Jeux d'eau* behind him.[1] Although the later set is, in general, denser in texture and harmony, the six piano pieces that comprise *Miroirs* and *Jeux d'eau* clearly come from the same hand and take essentially the same path to tone painting on the piano.

To listen to *Jeux d'eau* is to understand it, but this tightly woven, highly finished musical fabric is hard to explain to first-time listeners in part because analysis so easily risks robbing the work of its magic. What's most important to grasp is that Ravel coaxes sounds from the piano, mostly from the middle and upper range of the keyboard, that suggest the play of water in and light upon a fountain. Rather than fully developed melodies of the kind Liszt sets out in both of his aforementioned works, Ravel deploys thematic fragments and short, incisive phrases to give his piece substance and structure on which to drape the astonishing range of liquid sounds and keyboard-inspired figuration that convince listeners that they are not only hearing, but "seeing" the fountains with their ears. These figurations consist almost entirely of scales and arpeggios—broken chords—distributed, redistributed, and varied with high inventiveness and at dizzying speed.

As you listen, note the rocking figure at the beginning, as Ravel shifts meters freely, introducing a steady stream of subtle hiccups that tickle the ear. A strongly rhythmic unifying motto in the left hand is decorated by delicately dissonant ornamentation in the right. An accelerating passage leads to a swift climax on a high-set tremolo. Later, following another climactic cadenza-like passage, the rocking motif returns, decorated even more lavishly. Ravel's instruction "*sans ralentir*"—"don't slow down"—for the final scale before the end tells the performer not to sentimentalize the pictorial effects the composer has worked so hard to achieve, and the work ends on an open, mildly dissonant chord that gives an impression of water catching the light.

Sonatine

In musical terminology, a sonata is an instrumental composition of varying dimensions; perhaps most common is a three-movement format with the first and last in lively tempos and the middle at a contrasting slower pace. From the mid-eighteenth century on, a sonata takes on other implications regarding the forms and progression of each movement, with *sonata form* meaning something quite specific. As you might expect, a sonatina, or *sonatine*, as it's called in French, is a sonata made to smaller dimensions. Important composers, including Beethoven, have composed sonatinas as well as the big sonatas that are well known. The small dimensions of Ravel's *Sonatine*, begun in 1903 and completed two years later, fit comfortably into the sonatina category. Of course, his craftsmanship is as high in this great work as anywhere in his output, but the affects—the passions—it summons are anything but small in scale.

Only about four minutes long, the opening movement has a compressed sonata structure that will satisfy those who appreciate order and organization, but the material itself, beginning with the opening theme's falling interval followed by an impassioned, urgently rising phrase, all set over a fluttering accompaniment, speaks with an emotion that's barely in check; yet Ravel never gives up the delicacy and control that define his style. The more earthbound second theme (*long*-short-*long* . . .) presents a calmer tone, and the descending third theme, which the composer uses as his closing idea, is thoughtful, and even tender. Brief and pithy, the opening sequence is repeated. In the short passage that follows (known as the "development") Ravel stirs the three ideas together while turning up the heat, even using "*passioné*"—"passionately"—as an expression mark, bringing the passage to a swift climax on the second theme, which had seemed the calmest. The third section repeats the opening ideas in sequence, but compressed and with a reflective coda (closing passage) built on an exquisite blending of the first and third themes into phrases that alternately fall then rise.

A gentle minuet gives a few moments of dreamlike rest at the heart of the *Sonatine*. A delicate tune over a steady three-beat pulse opens the movement, followed by a contrasting idea that turns out to be a redeployed version of a mincing five-note phrase from the opening. Ravel builds these quiet elements into a grand rising phrase at the movement's center, then shifts keys at low volume, which makes the change sound strange and mysterious. He then contrives a quick but subtle return to the home key for the restatement of the main idea. The dreamy coda leads into a compressed version of the grand rising phrase, which closes the movement majestically. Henriette Faure, a pianist who studied the

Sonatine with Ravel, recalled that the composer loved the closing passage: "I will never forget the expression of grandeur he gave to the ascending melodic line, or the sudden radiance and authority of the final chord . . ."[2] This great evocation of the dance is a clear forerunner of the minuet of *Le Tombeau de Couperin*, where the composer works on a larger scale.

The flaring and rippling of the figuration that opens the headlong finale tells you right away that a real virtuoso is required here—it's much harder than the first two movements. It's exciting from start to finish, but Ravel continually holds back, lowering the volume and clouding the harmony. A sharp rhythm emerges from the fiery flow, followed closely by a reincarnation of the first movement's opening theme, slightly altered but unmistakable. Ravel marks the passage "*tranquille*"—"tranquil"—but the pleading urgency of the tune remains. A return of rushing passagework, expressed with abundant rhythmic hiccups that are a trademark of the master's style, introduce a discussion of the sharp figure between the hands. This leads in turn to the opening idea, now heard in a more veiled harmony. At once fervent and coolly distant, this backs a wonderful blending of the two ideas, one sharp edged, the other nostalgic. Once again the opening idea returns, as rushing passagework in excited, ever-tightening rhythmic contractions leads to the final chord. And typically for Ravel, it's mildly dissonant, exhilarating but open-ended.

Miroirs

"Mirrors," completed in 1905, with its suggestion of visual reflections, is one of the crucial works cast in this mold by both Ravel and Debussy in this extraordinary era, decade, and year for piano music in France. The two masters traded concepts for titles, and sometimes actual musical ideas, with Ravel often ahead on the conceptual front, as we'll see. Whether in competition, mutual appreciation, or both, the two spurred each other on. Debussy's *Estampes*—"Prints"—dates from 1903; his two sets of *Images*—"Images," obviously—from 1905 and 1907. While his two books of *Préludes* (1910 and 1913) are titled more neutrally, nearly each piece within the sets of twelve are takes on visual or aural ideas, wonderful examples of music that's inspired by the outside world.[3] All of the works mentioned here stand on their own, with no requirement that they be played together: for example, the *Alborada del gracioso* is the most popular and frequently performed of the five *Miroirs*.

The set opens, however, with the strange and beautiful *Noctuelles*, a sublime depiction of fluttering moths, an unlikely subject for poetic treatment. Ravel chose for his title an unusual word that names a species of moth, into which the suggestion of *nocturne* is embedded as well. While this is not precisely a nocturne in Chopin's sense, it has a dimly lighted, nocturnal quality. The delicate, very dissonant fluttering of the opening immediately evoke an image of moths batting around, and Ravel ends his opening paragraph with delicate scales and twitches that also suggest an insect's movements. This material is brought to a gentle climax on a high-set tremolando—a rapid alternation of repeated chords hands resulting in a brilliant sonority. (You heard one in *Jeux d'eau*.) The contrasting passage that follows, a bit slower and initially much less fluttery ("*sombre et expressif*" is the composer's expression mark), is darkly lyrical, in rich chords set against pulsing syncopated notes for the left hand, a pattern Ravel makes much use of in his works for piano from here on. Interrupted, at first occasionally, then more steadily by arpeggios and the opening passagework, but set lower on the keyboard, the chordal patterns eventually break apart. Within this transition, there's a passionate rising phrase over the pulsing of the left hand to listen for. The opening fluttering returns, and the final page contains one more loud tremolando, followed by a falling, cadenza-like passage, to be played very lightly, a reminiscence of the chordal passage, and a few last moments of fluttering, as though moving away.

Oiseaux tristes—"Sad Birds"—inverts the pattern of *Noctuelles*, its still and solemn outer portions contrasting with a (slightly) more active middle section. The piece opens with an imitation of song, supposedly a blackbird's. Studied, carefully phrased, and majestically poised, these opening three bars alone seem timeless. Chords that are almost suffocatingly heavy accompany still, solitary notes that, again, evoke with uncanny power the sound of birds calling in the distance. Ravel increases the movement in the middle section, with bird sounds that are more aggressive, some shrilly anticipating those in the *Petit Poucet* section of *Ma Mère l'Oye*. The majestic calls of the opening return, alongside a passionate suggestion of melody, above the slow-moving accompaniment from before. As in *Noctuelles*, a light-handed cadenza leads to the closing phrases, which are very dissonant, and marked by Ravel to sound "*sombre et lointain*"—"somber and distant." And as is normal for the composer, this great tone poem ends on an unresolved dissonance.

The longest piece in *Miroirs*, *Une Barque sur l'océan*—"A Boat on the Ocean"—comes across a bit like *Jeux d'eau* on steroids, as Ravel again renders the motions of water. Here, of course, the sea—swelling, splashing, spilling, and shifting—is the subject, and it's enormously powerful, though its keyboard textures are perhaps less varied than in the earlier work. Two fluid patterns emerge at the start, a falling figure in the right hand over seething arpeggios in the left. Ravel's rhythmic flexibility is impressive as he renders the sea's irregular motion with phrases that expand and contract freely without losing their impetus. Out of these a typically Ravelian open-ended melodic idea appears, then a sequence of tremolandos over continual arpeggios in the left, that capture the exhilaration, edged with terror, of being at sea. Thicker chords appear over and under the remarkably varied figuration, which hardly pauses over the seven minutes *Une Barque* takes to perform. The composer returns to the opening idea and to the tremolandos once more, as well as a dripping figure that he transforms into another rich, chordal phrase. A final run-through of the trembling phrases leads to a temporary slowdown over a stalking left hand; knowing a good idea when he has one, Ravel ends the piece with the gorgeous opening phrase, broken up and disembodied.

The most popular, structurally complex, and technically difficult piece in *Miroirs*, the *Alborada del gracioso* is also a landmark for the composer, opening a phase in which Spanish-influenced music remains on the front burner with the composition of the *Rapsodie espagnole* of 1907 and peaking with the opera *L'Heure espagnole* of 1909. The title, one of the composer's more difficult, translates clumsily as "The Jester's Morning Song." The jester in question—the *gracioso*—is a stock figure from Spanish stage comedy, funny but also biting in his humor. So, while the *Alborada* is the most humor-filled work in *Miroirs*, it's not entirely funny, containing unmistakable veins of bitterness and melancholy.

Exciting to hear but strenuous to perform, none of the other *Miroirs* matches the *Alborada* for difficulty. The *Alborada* contains every pianistic trap imaginable, from wide jumps to passagework that's rapid but needs to remain clear to achieve the effects Ravel intends. Perhaps most notorious among the pitfalls are its long passages of repeated notes. The heavy action of most American and German pianos only makes their execution harder, and here, as much as anywhere in the master's works for piano, it's important to understand that the instrument Ravel composed on and liked to play was a French-made Érard with a much lighter touch. So, even great virtuosos can sound uneven as they try to fire off the batteries of repeated tones on Steinways and Bösendorfers. Although the *Alborada* is rightly "regarded with terror by pianists,"[4] the performance of by Romanian artist Dinu Lipatti, who died in 1950 of leukemia at age thirty-three, still sets the standard for speed, accuracy, clarity, and elegance.

British pianist and musicologist Roy Howat has shown that Ravel wrote and developed the several themes of the *Alborada* with more careful calculation than you might expect, given its free-sounding character and headlong pace, but it's really not necessary to get into the nuts and bolts to sense that many of its ideas are related, or—surely not—to enjoy this brilliant work.[5] Just remember when you listen that, while wonderfully varied, the *Alborada* moves at terrifying speed, and that its apparent roughness is a calculated effect by the composer, whose technical skills place him among the most adroit and polished composers.

Opening with a spiky syncopated phase imitating the guitar, a melody into which a turn is embedded emerges, and from this a more ferocious incarnation of the turn. Soon the right hand is spitting out those infamous repeated notes, and, after a big flourish, there's a long, moody recitative-like passage, interspersed with high-set, repeated chords in flamenco rhythm as a contrasting background. Even if ironically layered, the affect here seems somber and urgent rather than high-spirited. Included in this passage is a falling turn Ravel would borrow a few years later for the final ensemble of *L'Heure espagnole*. The turns lead to a reiteration of the opening strumming, followed by hammered repeated notes and a stunning sequence of double glissandos, with two fingers sliding up and down the keys. The opening idea receives a more lyrical iteration, but Ravel fragments his material and mixes all together with ever-increasing velocity. The work climaxes on a strikingly dissonant rendering of a leaping theme, ending on a glittering snarl and a snap.

Inspired by the sounds of church bells in Paris, *La Vallée des cloches*—"The Valley of the Bells"—forms a rich and calm conclusion to *Miroirs*. And surely "The Great Gate at Kiev," the majestic closing section of Mussorgsky's *Pictures at an Exhibition*, in which that master evokes tolling bells, served as a kind of example and inspiration for Ravel, even though the two-tone paintings differ in affect and dynamics, with Mussorgsky's being mostly excited, exalted, and loud, whereas Ravel finds ecstasy in a quieter, less obvious way. Like Mussorgsky, Ravel gets the piano to sound like many bells, some pealing, others resounding deeply by using the sustain pedal to hold long tones while the hands move around the keyboard. To clarify his intentions for the player, he writes the score in three lines instead of the normal two.

The piece moves at one slow, even tempo, making the job easier on the performer. *La Vallée* opens quietly with repeated tones, into which a steady, murmuring carillon enters. A third set of "bells," these falling deeply and slowly in the left hand, come in. A long-breathed melody, marked "*très calme*" by the composer, opens the middle section, and from this a soaring, ecstatic melody emerges, accompanied throughout by a variety of chiming effects. The long-breathed melody is heard again, extended into even longer, falling phrases. The carillon returns in abbreviated form and at lower volume, then fragmented, and the piece ends quietly with two low chimes, sounded softly, deep in the left hand.

Gaspard de la nuit

Of all the titles in Ravel's catalog, this is probably the hardest to translate. Anyone who studied French in high school knows that *de la nuit* means "of the night," but to identify Gaspard requires a bit of background. *Gaspard de la nuit* is the title of the anthology of prose poems by Aloysius Bertand, published in 1842, one year after Bertrand's death. These sketches, which relate fantastical and mysterious tales about water sprites, the sighs of hanged men, spiteful gnomes, and the like, must have been influenced by the folktales retold by the brothers Grimm and the stories of German romantic writer E. T. A. Hoffmann; they're also contemporary with and close in spirit to those by Edgar Allan Poe. Described as a ragged old man, Gaspard is the nominal narrator of the sixty-three sketches that the poet has merely transcribed; Gaspard turns out to be the devil himself.[6] Ravel's musical renderings add at least one more layer of sophisticated ambiguity to Bertrand's narratives, which are already ironic, thanks to their supposedly satanic authorship. As with the Grimm and Poe tales, Bertrand's sketches are nightmarish and weirdly remote, and Ravel's rare ability to evoke distance in time is well matched to the material. The demonic power and difficulty of these three extraordinary interpretations of words into music will be obvious even to the first-time listener.

Completed in 1908, *Gaspard de la nuit* stands as one of the greatest works for piano by Ravel—or anyone. Its manifold beauties are matched by the famous difficulty of its third movement, *Scarbo*, but all three sections are hard to play, with each posing different technical challenges. The influence of Liszt is clear, particularly in *Scarbo*, which descends from that composer's great *Mephisto Waltz* No. 1. Schumann's *Kreisleriana*, a masterful, eight-movement keyboard suite inspired by E. T. A. Hoffmann, also anticipates *Gaspard*'s fantastical spirit and manic energy.

The narratives that inspire *Gaspard* make it "program" music, and Ravel selected the three poems that inspired the movements with an eye and ear for maximum contrast among them. While neither in sonata form nor "absolute" music, the work takes for its overall layout the fast-slow-fast sequence of which *Sonatine* is a good example. Ravel's suite is close in incident and even closer in spirit to the texts, with the score subtitled "Three poems for piano after Aloysius Bertrand." The first, *Ondine*, tells of a water sprite who tries to lure a mortal into the dangers of the stream where she lives. Taking her name from *onde*, the word for "wave," *Ondine* is the last and greatest of Ravel's three pianistic tone poems depicting water. The second, *Le Gibet*—"The Gallows"—asks a sequence of horrifying rhetorical questions about a body hanging on gibbet outside of a town and of a ringing that echoes; here, in what acts as the central panel of this triptych, the music moves slowly as Ravel paints his musical images with brave fidelity to the text. The third, *Scarbo*, takes the name of a malicious dwarf who maddens the narrator with his teasing and pranks. Here, in music of power and fearful difficulty, the composer captures the dwarf's unpredictable movements and alarming character. This movement combines features of a scherzo, a type of playful, quick-time music with the cathartic excitement of a finale. Unlike the five tone poems that make up *Miroirs*, the three of *Gaspard* need to be played and heard together, in sequence, with each essential to the balance and impact of whole.

There's no water sprite quite like Ravel's, but in another example of the two masters using each other for inspiration, Debussy also composed an *Ondine* as one of the elements in Book II of his *Préludes*, completed in 1913. Debussy's more sunlit view of the nymph is no slouch, however, and it's a great work you should listen to as well.

Ravel's *Ondine*, like that of Bertrand's poem, is a seductress who hides her treacherous nature behind a song of irresistible beauty. When you listen to the piece, remember that the composer builds it basically out of two elements: the gorgeous, haunting melody of the water sprite's lament, and a shimmering accompaniment that transforms itself as the music progresses. But even its first appearance at the opening of the *Gaspard* sets this accompaniment apart, bestowing on the work a tone and mood all its own. Where the typical figuration that accompanies a big melody moves in a predictable pattern at a steady pulse, this one shivers, its harmony eerie and ambiguous. Over the course of the piece, Ravel develops it with fantastic ingenuity and beauty, with more evolved versions of what he achieved in *Jeux d'eau* and *Une Barque sur l'océan*, including scales and arpeggios that at some points seem to splash and drip. Over this steals the perfect melody, long and supple. In fact, it's built of short phrases that the composer manipulates, lengthening, shortening, breaking into pieces, and moving over the keyboard as his development proceeds, none of which ever seems to take away from its unceasing, unbearable beauty. Ravel creates a sense of light's changing on the water, and the creature seems to slide away just under its surface more than once. The composer achieves these impressions with huge leaps between tonalities made at low volume. The music reaches a glorious climax on a version of the siren's song, then quiets just before the end as the bare melody is sounded, depicting her pleading, weeping, and sulking. In the final passages, Ondine regains her composure, laughs, then splashes and swims away as the flowing accompaniment sounds solemnly.

Bertrand's short prose poem *Le Gibet* quotes a line from Goethe's *Faust* at its head ("What do I see moving around that gibbet?"), to which it replies, first with six macabre rhetorical questions, then ending with the plain answer that the sound is the ringing of a bell from a city in the distance, and the sight that of a hanged man's "carcass reddening in the setting sun." Ravel uses these bleak images to create a tone poem of concentration and great, if terrible, beauty, making *Le Gibet* the most difficult of *Gaspard*'s three tone poems to grasp. The chiming effects of *La Vallée des cloches* from *Miroirs* stand as its direct forebear in sound and technique, though certainly not in mood.

Le Gibet also contrasts radically in texture from the busy, note-filled sections that flank it. The bell mentioned in the last line of the poem is heard as a soft tone that opens the piece, repeating continually through its six-minute playing time, and is the last sound we hear. For the rest, Ravel assembles a layered structure in which melodic elements pass through, typically stated in long, block chords, and the harmony attempts unsuccessfully to escape from the pull of that repeated tone, which itself can play havoc on the nerves of sensitive listeners. Next to *Ondine* and *Scarbo*, *Le Gibet* sounds easier to play, but the music presents different kinds of technical challenges, involving control, tempo, pacing, and touch. It's music that can easily sound boring in the hands of a mediocre player: the ability to get through the notes is no guarantee of a successful projection of the work's depths, beauties, ironies, and perils. Although Ravel depicts an awful monotony here, *Le Gibet* must not sound monotonous.

Le Gibet opens with that repeated note, a B-flat for those keeping track. Under this, a somber figure that's not quite a tune emerges in big chords in the left hand, then a wailing phrase in the right. The composer alternates, then extends the somber figure into a full, pain-filled melody that speaks of infinite loss and regret. We feel strangely sorry for the hanged man, even though we know nothing about him from the poem except that he's bald. Yet Ravel's music seems to set the scene from a great, indeed a majestic, distance. Although we may be far from the dreadful event related by Gaspard to the poet, and here retold musically, that music evokes our deepest pity.

In the middle section, an eerie, fiercely dissonant descending chord sequence illustrating one of the horrors mentioned in the text makes an assault on the repeated, nerve-wracking B-flat, but fails to budge it. Over a thinner texture, the wailing melody is brought back and extended, then the long, block chord tune, again summoning a generic but intense sorrow. The eerie falling chords come back over booming repeated notes deep in the bass, resounding like a different, deeper bell; the opening phrase of the long, block chord tune is repeated, and the repeated B-flats, as though suspended over nothing, finally trail off.

Scarbo, the closing section, is without question one of the most difficult pieces in the repertory. Here the influence of Liszt is most pronounced, with the mercurial tone and wild keyboard choreography descended from that master's *Mephisto Waltz* No. 1. Ravel also cited the Russian composer Mily Balakirev's fine but rarely performed showpiece *Islamey* as being of a technical difficulty he hoped to surpass.[7] Two more likely inspirations on the Russian side are the second of Mussorgsky's *Pictures at an Exhibition*, "Gnome," and the second-to-last, "The Hut on Hen's Legs" (Baba Yaga). As noted, *Scarbo* resembles a scherzo in its playfulness and a finale in its power and dramatic sweep, but for all the prodigious skill it demands, *Scarbo*, like the works by Liszt and Mussorgsky, is spooky fun: devilishly hard and thrilling when well performed, but ultimately not terrifying in the same way as *Le Gibet*.

Ravel builds *Scarbo* out of a number of varied thematic elements, some of which are presented as fragments, like the three-note figure sounded deep in the bass that opens the piece, which is soon extended into a longer arching phrase. You'll also hear drumming repeated notes, as in the *Alborada del gracioso*, here set under a crunching, dissonant chord. A busy five-note figure suggests the imp's manic energy, and uneasy hopping chords in an abrupt and decisive short-*long* pattern—probably the most important of *Scarbo*'s themes—that depict his sudden appearances and disappearances; these are interspersed with a buzzing figure that restlessly spins a single tone up and down the keyboard. The five-note phrase dominates the next passage, as the composer ratchets up the excitement by breaking the thematic ideas up and pushing the fragments ever closer together. Long, falling lines join the texture, and a big climax is reached on the five-note figure in a chattering incarnation and the arching phrase, played out over boiling arpeggios.

The furious movement seems to halt as the opening figures are recalled, now as though frozen. Very gradually, Ravel starts the motion again, restating the opening material quietly, then over a rising and falling scale that repeats deep in the bass. Alarming tremolandos and trills reintroduce the five-note phase in a stretched-out form, followed by a long, difficult transition to the crucial short-long motto. Ravel builds this into an enormous crescendo, interspersed with fast, savage chords between the hands. The final pages include reiterations of the arching theme and the broadened version of the five-note phrase. Ravel closes *Scarbo* by sounding the three-note figure from the opening under a weirdly harmonized tremolo, ending on a low, sulfurous sputter.

Ma Mère l'Oye for Piano, Four Hands

Ravel composed this, the original version of *Ma Mère l'Oye* between 1908 and 1910, expanding and connecting its five movements for the orchestral suite, then the ballet that he completed two years later. Since all the music in the ballet is contained here, and to avoid redundancy, it's fully described in chapter 7 (pages 95–100). But, as is normal for Ravel, the earlier version stands entirely on its own merits, not merely as a sketch for the orchestral score. You'll be surprised by how charmingly the colors come through, even comparing the keyboard version with the brightly orchestrated *Laideronnette, impératrice des pagodes*. Don't miss this jewel of the repertory for four hands at one keyboard.

Menuet sur le nom d'Haydn

In 1909 Ravel and other French composers, including Debussy, were commissioned to write works in tribute to Haydn, the centenary of whose death was that year. Applying the letters attached to musical tones, Ravel composed this exquisite, if isolated, mini-masterpiece, his "Minuet on the Name of Haydn." He works the classical era master's name through the two-page score at least six times, inverting and reversing it as well as running it straight ahead. When you listen, you'll be struck not by Ravel's cleverness at applying learned compositional techniques; rather, by its beauty and its nostalgic feel, the latter achieved by the application of the gently dissonant harmonies that are a fingerprint of his mature style, and noticeable right from the opening.

Valses nobles et sentimentales

The ancestry and background of this pivotal 1911 work (CD Track 2) are long and complex. The title, "Noble and Sentimental Waltzes," may not require translation, but some explanation is called for. From straight on, it's a take-off on the waltz suites of Schubert, one of which is called the *Valses sentimentales* and another the *Valses nobles*. The personalities of both sets differ slightly, with the former a bit more tender and perhaps "feminine," and the latter more proud and "masculine," if you'll allow the old-fashioned descriptors. While considered minor in the context of Schubert's output, they are charming, likable, and fun to hear. Unlike Ravel, Schubert used the titles without irony; Ravel modeled his work clearly on and in tribute to Schubert's dance suites. But alongside Ravel's *Valses nobles*, Schubert's waltzes are studies in innocence. Ironies are already implicit, beginning with the fact that Schubert wrote his to be danced to, but Ravel did not (except in their orchestrated and choreographed version). The *Valses nobles* mark a turn away from the opulence and passion of *Gaspard* to a lighter, cooler, more objective style; and like all of Ravel's work, they steer completely clear of sentimentality. They anticipate both *La Valse* and his final keyboard masterpiece, *Le Tombeau de Couperin*. If dissonances could be measured, *Gaspard* and the *Valses nobles* are probably equal, but the thinner textures of the later work expose them more clearly, and to its first audiences, painfully.

Many sources in addition to Schubert nourished Ravel's imagination. Well-known piano works by Schumann and Chopin inspired him, too. One of Schumann's earliest works, the *Papillons*, is a take on a Schubert waltz suite, but like the *Valses nobles* it's ripe with ambiguous and ironic echoes. Techniques and methods in Schumann's better-known piano works *Carnaval* and *Davidsbündlertänze* clearly influenced Ravel's themes and keyboard writing in several ways and places, as we'll see; and Chopin's waltzes also had a significant impact. From a formal standpoint, many of Chopin's waltzes, perhaps most obviously the *Grande Valse brillante*, Op. 18, are in fact suites of dances, and Ravel put to good use in the *Valses nobles* some of Chopin's rhythmic subtleties, even copying Chopin's distinctive way of notating one such trick. Like many serious composers, Ravel admired the elegant, idealized waltz suites of Johann Strauss.

As you may have gathered, dissonance—the sound of tones that clash to the ear—is a key to the beauty of the *Valses nobles*, but they came across as incomprehensibly bare and harsh to its initial audience. In one sense, the history of Western music is the story of the advancement of dissonance by composers and its acceptance by audiences. All great composers, from the late medieval masters on, used dissonance freely, and as a general rule before the twentieth century, the greater the composer, the bolder he was in employing dissonance, continually pushing limits and finding new ways to work it in. (I'm excluding the twentieth century on, only because with one or two exceptions it's not fully clear whose music will last.) They did this because dissonance is one of the most powerful expressive weapons in any composer's armory, and in this respect, Ravel did his share. It's hard for modern listeners to believe that his gorgeous music could ever be perceived as difficult, but that's because we hear him in the context of works by Stravinsky, Schoenberg, Webern, Varèse, Boulez, and many others who in the twentieth century aggressively pushed dissonance well beyond Ravel. "Tonal, but with a lot of wrong notes," is how the pianist Bernard Rose described the harmonic scheme of the *Valses nobles*, where the composer's sophisticated strategy is to chisel away the expected notes, rigorously avoiding the trite and expected. One or more tunes are present in every one of these eight strange little dances, but be sure to listen for those wrong notes, which you might perceive, depending on the context, either as acid etching or a citric brightness that's present throughout.

The familiarity of the waltz rhythm will help many listeners, and its structure is relatively straightforward, a sequence of seven short waltzes, independent but tied, that alternate in mood, followed by a dreamlike epilogue. The first waltz opens with a bold statement in a fiery short-short-long rhythmic pattern set in big, dissonance-laced chords. A more sweeping figure takes over, containing several of Ravel's characteristic rhythmic hiccups. The sweeping figure dominates the brief middle section, and big chords lead back to a statement of the bold opening idea. The second dance is a dreamy and delicate mix of falling first theme and a rising second. Ravel copies several of Chopin's waltzes by decorating the second theme with grace notes dropping from high above. The lively and almost cheerful third waltz is a good example of the beauty of Ravel's harmonic subtlety with every other chord in the lilting opening part being charged with dissonance, but to an effect that's clean and bracing. Sun-drenched but tart chords set over hiccups dominate the middle section, and the rhythm at the end anticipates the swaying main theme of the elusive fourth waltz. Here, too, there's hardly a plain chord to be found, as scurrying triplets animate its movement.

The slower fifth waltz sets a tender falling melody inspired by Schumann's manner over a richly chromatic accompaniment, while the very short middle section presents a rhythmic game where Ravel sets a two-beat melody against the three-beat waltz rhythm. And the closing bars again evoke Schumann, notably the more lyrical sections of the bipolar *Davidsbündlertänze*. The bounding opening of the sixth dance forms a strong contrast with what it follows, balanced later by more reflective phrases. The seventh waltz opens with a dreamy passage, as though heard from a distance, which soon gains focus and energy, anticipating a similar procedure in *La Valse*. Here, in the most thunderous passage after the opening, a generously phrased waltz finally emerges in harmonically unambiguous radiance. The note-spinning of the lighter-textured middle section copies Chopin's *Grande valse*, Op. 42, where again a melody phrased in two notes dangles gracefully though very dissonantly over a fluid waltz rhythm; it's here that Ravel borrows Chopin's notation. The big waltz returns to end the piece with high energy.

Dreamy and smoky, the *Épilogue* suggests waltz rhythms, and even summons ghostly recollections of most of the preceding dances, but these pass as Ravel ends this compact masterpiece in ambiguity and uncertainty. The misty atmosphere and nostalgic tone, with material from earlier in the work recalled, of the final two sections of the *Davidsbündlertänze* surely anticipate the mood and structure of Ravel's closing, as does the gravitational pull of a softly repeated tone deep in the bass, to be found on the closing pages of both compositions.

Prélude

The first of three short keyboard works written in 1913, this elegant, minute-long study is built on a twisting, evocatively harmonized theme over rising figures in the left hand. The melody takes on more urgency before fading to end on a rising arpeggio and a characteristic floating dissonance. Although much longer and thicker in texture than Ravel's, Chopin's solitary Prelude in C-sharp Minor, Op. 45, may have set the tone for this perfect two-page summary of the Ravelian musical vocabulary.

À la Manière de . . . Emmanuel Chabrier [In the Style of Emmanuel Chabrier; Paraphrase on a melody by Gounod]

Ravel's ironic manner is on display in the first of two studies on other composers' styles. This one is actually a double paraphrase, taking a melody from Gounod's opera *Faust* and treating it as Chabrier might have done. This involves decorating it with richly chromatic harmony and setting it in widespread keyboard textures. Listening may well make you think about exploring the underappreciated Chabrier's oeuvre.

À la Manière de . . . Borodine (Valse) [In the Style of Alexander Borodin (Waltz)]

Ravel captures the Russian composer's melodic style with uncanny skill in this three-part work, which opens with a lilting, really Borodin-like tune over a droning accompaniment, before skittering off into a more flighty section that expands rather grandly considering the work's modest proportions, with the composer's even marking its climax to be played passionately. Ravel then brings back the opening idea, which he then blends with the flighty waltz, ending this remarkable study quietly.

Le Tombeau de Couperin

The title of Ravel's final work for the piano follows French musical tradition: *tombeau* means "tomb," with as a second, figurative sense, a posthumous tribute. François Couperin (1668–1733) was one of the greatest composers of the French baroque, whose music, including that for keyboard, combines grace, charm, and unexpected lyrical depths, inspiring Ravel, Debussy, and Richard Strauss, among many others. Couperin belongs to a school of French composers referred to as the *clavecinistes*—which translates awkwardly as "keyboardists"—who played and composed for the harpsichord and clavichord. Their works often have descriptive titles that sometimes, though not inevitably, suggest people, animals, or nature, or a technical challenge they contain.

This underexplored category contains an astonishing range of music that's good and great; like Ravel, Debussy revered his French musical forebears. *Hommage à Rameau*—"Homage to Rameau," from the first set of *Images*—is one of Debussy's most profound keyboard works. *Hommage* similarly evokes another eighteenth-century master, Jean-Philippe Rameau, and is itself a type of *tombeau*, or tribute; like Ravel's, it's elegiac rather than tragic in mood. Two of Debussy's collections for piano, the *Suite bergamasque* of 1890 and *Pour le piano* of 1901, are tributes to the earlier masters' forms, written in Debussy's early postromantic idiom. And Debussy and Ravel were hardly alone on this bandwagon, with other French composers, including Fauré, Chabrier, Dukas, and later Poulenc, looking to eighteenth-century masters, including Bach and Scarlatti, for inspiration.[8]

Ravel's suite functions as a tribute in several ways. Obviously it's an homage to Couperin and the other *clavecinistes*, but also to the French compositional schools of the seventeenth and eighteenth centuries, and more broadly to French music, at a time when France and Germany (with its associated heavier, more convoluted musical styles) were at war. It's also a memorial to six of the composer's friends and acquaintances who died in World War I, to whom the work's six movements are individually dedicated.

The six movements of *Le Tombeau de Couperin* follow forms freely adapted from baroque instrumental suites, such as the partitas for keyboard by Bach. Ravel's suite opens with a bustling prelude in a fingery keyboard style, then a delicate fugue. Three dance movements follow: a *Forlane* and a *Menuet* that are dreamy in character, with a well-known and energetic *Rigaudon* in between. The suite ends with a very difficult *Toccata*, another showy form adapted from the baroque. The affects of *Le Tombeau de Couperin* are many and varied within each of its six movements, safe though it may be to describe its governing sense as elegiac. Typically enough, veins of emotion run just beneath the master's elegantly austere surfaces, though these may not always be easy to identify with dead accuracy. Ravel's keyboard style here follows the trail blazed in the *Valses nobles*: clean, clear, with the acid-etched harmonic language that is entirely the composer's own. While the six movements follow a carefully gauged arc, some of the movements have found life apart from the complete set, particularly the four that Ravel orchestrated and rearranged to end with the *Rigaudon*. Certainly the *Forlane* and *Rigaudon* are the most widely familiar, with the former often cited as the high point of *Le Tombeau*. This has led to speculation that the fugue is not up to the rest, while others feel the *Toccata* a letdown; in fact, its clearly pianistic style made it less adaptable by Ravel to orchestration. And although introverted, the fugue seems well up to its sublime company, simply asking more of the listener. Although it's one of the high points of Ravel's achievement, *Le Tombeau* is rarely performed in recital, though one or two movements show up on occasion as encores. The infrequency may be explicable in part by the fact that the concluding *Toccata* is much harder to play than what it follows. But while fairly familiar, this enchanting, ultrasophisticated masterpiece really cries out to be performed and heard live.

Perhaps the most closely tied to the style of Couperin and the other *clavecinistes*, the opening *Prélude* is notable for its busy, steady perpetual motion that never seems heavy. Based on two ideas, a spinning figure that opens the piece, then later a rising thematic idea, the piece buzzes along on its own mysterious energy, with its manifold beauties revealing themselves gradually but inevitably. As he does so often, the composer builds thematic elements from short, repeated phrases, which here, as usual, he later extends into long, arching lines. Ravel achieves his burnished harmonic palette in several ways. A three-note turn is repeated many times, blurring slightly the clean lines and light textures where the ten fingers rarely hit more than three keys at a time. Along the same lines, Ravel achieves his effects with fingers, hands, and wrists, with only one instruction to use the sustain pedal, and that at the very end. Of course, pianists may pedal here and there, but discretion is required, as these thin textures are easily muddied. Ravel also moves between two keys that share the same key signature of one sharp (E minor and G major), with the minor key dominating but shifting freely and often to the major with the effect of sunlight cutting through clouds. Ravel keeps the dynamics—the volume—mostly on the low to moderate side, ending the piece on a rising scale and a shimmering tremolando that's one of his favorite devices, going back to *Jeux d'eau*.

Beautiful but enigmatic, the *Prélude*'s affects are not easily put into words. The dry tone and light textures suggest a thoughtful, objective posture. But its steady motion suggests an irresistible life force; and, as the spinning figure morphs into a long, rising melody over fluctuating harmony, a joy that isn't far from ecstasy may be heard in the last, long trajectory of these organically related themes.

The *Fugue* that follows is the most reticent of the suite's six movements and will be the hardest for the first-time listener to grasp. Fugue is a contrapuntal process in which a theme called the subject is played off against itself in a horizontal manner, different from the melody with accompaniment typical of most music. The word *counterpoint* may sound alarmingly strict and dull, but a strong contrapuntal technique can provide a skilled composer with strategies that are enriching rather than burdensome. Johann Sebastian Bach is the most famous master of fugal style, and still probably the greatest, but more composers that you might imagine (including Chopin, Schumann, and Verdi) deploy counterpoint outside of fugues to strengthen the structural underpinnings of their music.

One of Ravel's most inward-looking conceptions, the *Tombeau* fugue is a serious affair, conceived and executed with just a few concessions to soften its austerity. The best way to approach it is to take your time and let it settle in, as ultimately it should. It's in three voices (contrapuntal lines, not human voices). This also means that the texture is light, with only one, two, but never more than three notes played at one time. The subject, a hesitant, falling idea with three slight pauses built in, is of a chaste beauty. To contrast with its halting quality, the composer devises a countersubject with a built-in triplet to charge the rhythm a bit, moving things along. He also sets the piece mostly in the middle and upper-middle range of the keyboard, adding to its fragility. Fugues contain what are called episodes, where the subjects are subjected to different treatments, and about midway through, you'll hear one as the composer makes the falling subject rise. Toward the end, the subject and countersubject seem to cluster more thickly; these are known as *stretti*, where the material is made to enter in closer sequence.

Ravel studied a *forlane* by Couperin before composing his, and it's fair to assume he knew the one in Bach's Orchestral Suite No. 1. Both baroque masters' dances are more driving than Ravel's lovely, languid specimen. In Ravel's *Forlane*, easy-sounding melodies and sculpted harmony play off one other, but it's the graceful lilt of the 6/8 beat that drives the music. This little dance displays all Ravel's qualities, including his ability to evoke mixed, slightly ambiguous affects, perhaps describable as nostalgia with a melancholy tinge, delivered in a weightless package. Although this is complex music, you should have no difficulty in grasping its beauty the first time you listen.

Like many dance pieces under one title, the *Forlane* is actually a little suite of linked, complementary dances, the first beginning with a lilting tune in the right hand, set over chords that are dissonant but mellow; what seem like regular phrase lengths soon stretch into relaxed extensions, ending coolly in an antique-sounding cadence. Every element in the thematic sequence that follows comes clothed in different incarnations of the 6/8 beat. The second, for example, starts with the hands widely separated, with the right skipping down from a high perch, to which a more ardent phrase containing a little turn replies. The next theme, a droning tune set over its swaying rhythm, has a more temporizing quality, as it's punctuated by repeated turns then commented on by playful scampering high on the keyboard. Ravel brings back the opening idea, slightly altered, followed by one last skipping dance, set in the center of the keyboard, then higher up in a more ecstatic incarnation. The closing page of this miraculous movement winds things down gracefully, but spiced with dissonances that are rather more pungent.

The energetic and relatively straightforward *Rigaudon* that follows is one of Ravel's most famous pieces. Its bright, brisk affect and bustling keyboard writing once more recall the *clavecinistes*, as here, too, he borrows form from Couperin, Rameau, and nineteenth-century Norwegian composer Edvard Grieg, whose *Holberg Suite* features another fine and well-known specimen. This rustic dance movement opens with a musical joke, an emphatic statement that's actually a closing cadence, making the piece sound as though it's over before it gets going. This dance movement speaks in more resolute, less ambiguous tones than any of *Tombeau*, at least until a transitional passage where a reduction in volume and Ravel's ineffable harmonic setting suggests a more intimate, still joyous emotion. The middle section features an angular melody in the tonic minor key, but remains cheerful before shifting back toward the opening tonality. A condensed restatement of the opening leads to the first phrase, which here finds its proper place, ending the movement.

With the gentle, dreamy *Menuet* the composer returns to higher spiritual ground, with the minuet of the *Sonatine* standing as its unmistakable ancestor. In a standard three-part form, the outer sections consist of a sublime dance tune that comes across almost as fragile. Ravel emphasizes its delicacy by reiterations in the upper middle range of the keyboard, and by using less dissonance here than in any other section of the suite. The middle section is designated by the composer as a *Musette*, which means that it should contain a bagpipelike droning and, theoretically at least, little harmonic movement. But its minor key, booming bass notes, and big, chromatic chords unmistakably suggest menace, perhaps of war, more clearly than any passage in the suite. Soon the *Menuet* melody floats back over the retreating chords. The *Menuet* tune finally returns in its plain glory, then transfigured over a rocking accompaniment. Ravel ends the movement with unusual, tranquilly rustling trills in both hands.

The *Toccata* that concludes the suite looks back to a form that originated in baroque Italy as a showpiece for skilled players to demonstrate their touch, *toccare*. Bach composed many such works, all brilliant and difficult, for harpsichord and for organ. Ravel's *Toccata* follows this pattern, while characteristically mixing delicacy and climactic triumph in with the brilliance. The interplay of themes suggests sonata form, while the master's subtle harmonic colorings blur the edges of what might otherwise turn into an aggressive pounding of keys, à la Prokofiev, who also composed a work in the form. The movement is also the most technically difficult in *Tombeau*, with much overlapping of hands and long passages of repeated notes that recall the *Alborada del gracioso* and *Scarbo*, as well as flowing passages that show the presence of the composer of water pieces from *Jeux d'eau* to *Ondine*. Unlike these, however, this is abstract music, with no descriptive agenda.

The *Toccata* opens with quick, light, drumming figures shared by the hands, which evolve into a more urgent motoric figure, the first of its three themes. The second, a more delicate, breathless theme, appears in the right hand, followed again by the quasi-mechanical chattering; the third tune, is of long-limbed, liquid beauty, accompanied by quick but lacy passage work. Ravel develops the first and third themes in a tense but exciting discussion, saving the second for the movement's enormous, glittering, ecstatic climax.

4 Ravel and the Art of Transcription

The category of transcriptions forms a sizable, significant portion of Ravel's output. Since he composed at the piano, everything in this category began as a keyboard work that he transcribed for the orchestra, some sooner, others later. There's also a smaller group of works by other composers—most important are those by Mussorgsky and Debussy—reworked by Ravel; in a singular instance he transcribed Debussy's orchestral masterpiece *Prélude à l'après-midi d'un faune* for two pianos. It seems fair to assume that Ravel's readiness to transcribe grew out of the difficulty he experienced in composing, which as we've seen, increased painfully over the course of his career. Perhaps he just wanted to get as much mileage out of a piece, once written, as possible. In some cases he added story lines to piano works, and with so much of his music in dance form, he passed a fair amount along to choreographers for staging.

His skill as an orchestrator marks this crossover category as of higher interest than you might guess: it's not busy- or hackwork, and it provides a useful look a Ravel as a working professional. There's no question of authenticity, either, as with several posthumous transcriptions by others of *Gaspard de la nuit*; these are all from the composer's own pen. If you're making a project of learning Ravel's music, you simply need to hear everything. After that, you can begin to decide whether you like one version more than another, your own critical privilege. I'll mention what's behind my prejudice for the piano as we go, but there's nothing to question or doubt whatever your preference. In some instances, such as *La Valse*, the orchestral version is clearly the one that fulfills the music's potential; while in others, such as *Ma Mère l'Oye*, both for piano and orchestra are certainly equally fine.

Menuet antique

Ravel orchestrated this piece from 1895 almost thirty-five years later, in 1929. Reworked at the height of his mature powers, the orchestral version is lush, punchy, and lavish next to the piano original. He assigns the grandiose opening theme to sharp-edged strings and brass, and the droning melody of the middle section to winds. He also expands the central section with fanfares for muted brass.

Pavane pour une infante défunte

The differences in mood and affect between the original and the orchestrated version of 1910 are considerable, with the orchestral version sounding sadder, even mournful. The noble opening melody is assigned to the French horns and bassoons over pizzicato strings. The string section covers the second melody, making it sound more fragile than in the original, and the strings and harps add luscious swoops. The final iteration of the opening melody is given to the violins gently backed by flutes and oboe, with the harp taking the lutelike figuration. This transcription shows as well as anything can that the piano is a percussion instrument; some may miss its metallic tone and the greater sense of generalized emotion and ironic distance it provides.

Miroirs: *Une Barque sur l'océan*; *Alborada del gracioso*

Ravel transcribed two of the *Miroirs* for orchestra, *Une Barque* and the *Alborada del gracioso*; only the latter is sill performed with any frequency, although both can be listened to online. The transcriptions were made years apart, with that of *Une Barque* dating to 1907, and the *Alborada* to 1918. But the composer gives these pieces, already colorful on the keyboard, the full resources of his orchestral thinking. The orchestral version of the *Alborada* also benefits from coming after the *Rapsodie espagnole* and *L'Heure espagnole*, to both of which its kinship is obvious. The comical yet still urgent Spanish flavored mock-recitative originated in the piano version of the *Alborada* before migrating to *L'Heure espagnole*, where a bassoon covers similar material. The wild ending of the *Feria* from the *Rapsodie espagnole*, much like the conclusion of the 1905 piano version of the *Alborada*, also echoes here. It benefits as well from the master's brilliant but light touch with percussion, here represented with a large contingent, which you'll hear in its fullest bloom in *Daphnis et Chloé*. The *Barque* transcription, where the boiling keyboard figuration is spread across the orchestra, makes the music sound utterly different. It may remind you of Debussy's contemporaneous symphonic masterwork *La Mer*, which has three movements and so is larger in scale. What's missing in both of Ravel's orchestral expansions is the excitement to be found in hearing one musician's mastering difficult material.

Valses nobles et sentimentales

Ravel transcribed his 1911 keyboard masterwork for orchestra the following year. To this he added a plot for a ballet, titled *Adélaïde, ou le langage des fleurs*—"Adelaide, or the Language of Flowers." Set in Paris about 1820, his scenario involves the courtesan Adélaïde and rival suitors for her love, reminiscent of Verdi's *La traviata*. The ballet was performed many times in the years that followed, but has since fallen from favor. In the orchestral version of the *Valses nobles*, Ravel subtly enriches harmonies and of course the textures are necessarily fuller with the orchestra, again with a large but unobtrusive percussion section. Woodwinds are used with great beauty and subtlety as they pass melodic material around. The anticipations of *La Valse* in the thunderous passages of the seventh waltz are striking: you can really hear how the later tone poem got started. Ravel's impeccable expansion of the *Valses nobles* can't be criticized, but some simply prefer the work on the piano, where its harmonic edginess seems to come through more comprehensibly. But you'll want to get to know both versions.

There's no question that *La Valse* finds its fullest expression in the brilliant orchestrated version of 1920. The composer composed the work initially on the piano, then transcribing it for two keyboards, the latter version representing the piece powerfully as well, especially in a blazing 1982 recording made by the virtuosos Martha Argerich and Nelson Freire, which must be heard if at all possible.

Le Tombeau de Couperin

In 1920, Ravel orchestrated four of the piano suite's six movements, changing their order to achieve a better flow. The four movements set are the *Prélude*, the *Forlane*, the *Menuet*, and the *Rigaudon*, placed in that new order, thus ending with the most energetic of the piano suite's dance movements. Like the *Valses nobles*, the three dance movements were also choreographed, with the *Prélude* reserved as overture to a *Tombeau* ballet. The most obvious negative to the orchestral suite is the loss of the *Fugue* and *Toccata* from the piano version. Certainly, though, the orchestrated movements are rendered with the lightest touch imaginable and beautifully done. Here the composer uses a smaller orchestra, consisting of strings, woodwinds in pairs, two horns, one trumpet, and a harp; there is no percussion, contrabassoon, or heavy brass instruments. The woodwinds, particularly the sweet-toned oboe, are used with Mozartian finesse, as Ravel passes his melodic material between its paired families. In the *Menuet*, here switched to third place, the gentle tones of the flute and the English horn share melodic burden with the oboe; the central section, called *Musette* in the piano version, lacks that name in this version. Here it may be that the menace suggested by the bass notes in the piano version is missed, as the softer orchestral textures lack the piano's boom and percussive bite. The sharp-edged melody of the *Rigaudon*'s middle section is shared by the oboe and English horn in their lower, more plangent registers, and the tune itself seems tailor-made for these woodwinds. Again, apart from the lack of two movements, there's nothing to criticize in the orchestrated *Tombeau* suite. Some simply prefer the piano's edgier timbre and linear clarity.

Pictures at an Exhibition

It's hard to think of two composers who seem less alike than the rugged natural genius Mussorgsky and the conservatory-polished

Ravel. Yet as we know, Ravel adored Mussorgsky's work, learning much from the Russian's proto-impressionist freedom. Mussorgsky's works have endured all manner of editorial intervention, some entirely necessary, as where the technically deficient Russian made errors in basic notation. Other instances, such as Rimsky-Korsakov's rich reorchestration of *Boris Godunov*, are now coming into question, with reversion to Mussorgsky's thinner but nonetheless effective original score achieving more frequent performance. In 1922, at the request of conductor Serge Koussevitzky, Ravel undertook an orchestration of Mussorgsky's potent masterwork for piano, which he knew and revered. But the nature of Koussevitzky's commission required Ravel to put aside at least part of his reverence, as he had to bring all of his sophisticated orchestral technique to bear on the project.

Ravel's instinct for making the daring sound natural can be heard in "The Old Castle," where the saxophone (an instrument probably unknown to Mussorgsky) takes the melody. Ravel's freedom and subtlety with percussion were also foreign to the Russian, with Ravel's triangles and gongs sounding alien to Mussorgsky's style. But only a grouch would deny the enjoyment that listening to Ravel's scoring provides. It's likely that Ravel's version has declined from the enormous popularity it once had, but it's still a remarkable exercise that stands on its own merits and is fun and at moments awe-inspiring, just like the original.

5 The Concertos

Ravel's two concertos, both for piano, were composed simultaneously. Both begun in 1929, the *Concerto pour la main gauche*—the Concerto for the Left Hand—was finished the following year; the Piano Concerto in G Major, for two hands, was completed in 1931. Their contemporaneous creation forced—or perhaps allowed—the master to shape them of distinct character, which in most ways they are. The composer's task in the work for one hand was to make the piano sound as though two hands were at work. As a result, the solo part is elaborate and difficult; the orchestration is rich and heavy, and while its affects are varied, the concerto is one of Ravel's most serious and dramatic compositions. Formally it's unusual for being cast in a single, dense movement.

Its G major companion is certainly lighter, brighter, and more cheerful; the keyboard writing is open and easier, but still brilliant and strictly for professionals. Its form is a traditional three movements, with a quick first and third flanking a slow and lyrical central section. Orchestral textures are of a corresponding lightness, and high comedy reigns in the outer movements. As you get to know both masterworks, you'll find the composer's craftsmanship to be at its typical high level; you also may perceive that they share a driving impetus common to Ravel throughout his career, and an underlying seriousness of purpose, even in the work for two hands. Some critics feel that, especially in the G Major Concerto, Ravel's organic problem with active creation begins to appear.[1] But its opening movement, with its five fully developed themes, satisfies most listeners; and while the remainder of the work shows influence of Mozart, Stravinsky, and others, these seem fully metabolized into Ravel's own style. Theses paired concerti demonstrate why listeners want to think skeptically concerning generalizations about stylistic characteristics of Ravel's different periods. Late Ravel is supposed to be thin, dry, and playful; but the *Concerto pour la main gauche* is both one of his latest and richest scores; and there's nothing trivial about the Piano Concerto in G Major. While certainly playful for long stretches, the work has a lyrical heart and a spine of steel.

Concerto pour la main gauche

Ravel wrote this on a commission from the Austrian pianist Paul Wittgenstein. A brother of the philosopher Ludwig, Wittgenstein had lost his right arm in World War I, and commissioned left-hand works from several composers, including Ravel and Sergey Prokofiev. A difficult character—probably for good reason—Wittgenstein must have possessed a strong technique to go along with a mile-wide contrary streak. He and Ravel feuded over how to perform the piece, with Wittgenstein making changes that infuriated Ravel. Over the years, Wittgenstein came around, admitting that Ravel had been correct, and making the concerto a key element in his repertory.

Ravel's goal in writing a concerto for one hand was to make up in density what was lost to the sound of two. Thus, whereas the G Major Concerto is mostly light and cheerful, this one is powerful and thick in texture. Most of the notes are written for the middle and lower parts of the keyboard, for the obvious reason that that's the side where a player's left hand will be, but also because the lower notes have a louder and richer sound that carries better. But Ravel did players of this work no favors: it's one of the most difficult pieces in the repertory for one hand, if not the hardest. The keyboard throughout is, as noted, thick and complex, with the left hand playing both melody and accompaniment; so complete is the illusion that a first-time listener would never be in doubt if told that two hands were playing. The orchestration is also rich and dark, particularly alongside the bright sounds of the G Major Concerto. The scoring is for a full late-romantic orchestra, with brass and percussion sections of notable size and weight, pitted against the one-handed soloist, who must at times override it in volume, even as his technique and stamina are challenged by the difficulty of getting through its tangle of notes. More than just an exception to the thinner textures Ravel favored after World War I, this late-period work stands among the richest of his scores. The composer finds his own way to evoke the struggle typical of instrumental concertos of the classical and romantic eras, some of which are half-jokingly described as being for "piano against orchestra." Here, as with many of those, the soloist clearly represents an idealized individual battling the orchestral crowd.

With bewildering skill, Ravel turns our expectations upside down for what a work for one hand can achieve. In addition to the unexpected opulence of its sound, the concerto is a work of wit, in which the composer plays on multiple paradoxes to achieve his aesthetic goals. For example, although the piece has a typical playing time of only about eighteen minutes, it's eventful and satisfying. Along the same lines, despite its brevity, the concerto seems spacious and unhurried, with only a couple of passages that rush ahead. At a more textural level, its affects are more varied than you might expect, as Ravel invests its two most important themes—the heroic opening idea and the energetic march—with unexpected shadings. The primary theme, though unquestionably epic in character, also displays tender and reflective sides, and the march has a dizzying expressive spectrum, from aggressive to jazzily danceable, with other inflections that are harder to pin down in between. He also plays with the standard concerto structure, as he reverses the normal sequence of movements, or in this case, sections, from fast-slow-fast to slow-fast-slow. Casting the concerto into a single piece but subdivided into recognizable formal divisions that are performed without interruption, Ravel manages to squeeze in a scherzolike passage, as well as an intense sonata form development section.

The concerto opens with a murky group of low strings—cellos and double basses—that support a solo by perhaps the strangest sounding instrument in the orchestra, the contrabassoon. (Less afraid of its bizarre tone than many composers, Ravel employs it occasionally and effectively without overusing it.) The timbres are so shadowed that, until you know the piece well, you won't be able to grasp what you're hearing. Its weird growling is actually the work's chief theme, here submerged in the darkest orchestral timbre and textures. Although hard to make out, the theme is a broad melodic idea dominated by a jagged and exciting "dotted" rhythm: short-*long*. As the master often does when evoking mystery, he veils the theme, presenting it in embryonic form. Here he's saving its fully developed presentation for the soloist.

Very gradually, Ravel brightens the sounds, as at first moaning horns, bassoons, and a low-lying clarinet part join. But even as he's adding light, he's also thickening the textures. The entrance of the English horn signals a new phase in the thematic exposition, as violins and higher woodwind instruments finally join, the harmony setting a mood of high tension and anticipation. Note that Ravel devotes two to three minutes of this short work to this extraordinary introduction, with the piano yet to play a note. The soloist enters in a thunderous, minute-long cadenza; it's just the first of many fiercely difficult demonstrations of the virtuosity required of the soloist, and leading at last to the presentation of the chief theme, outlined by the contrabassoon at the start. Now we hear it in daylight, as it were, at once heroic and sublime, presented in full harmony and with big jumps for the hand over the keyboard. Long, difficult runs interrupt the melodic material with increasing frequency, including an unusual one marked by the composer to be played "*strepitoso*"—"noisily." The full orchestra joins the piano in an extended and exalted presentation of the epic theme. As this moves toward its final phrases, trumpets and horns chatter in triumphant commentary.

The tempo slows as the composer begins a densely written lyrical section, the long opening phrase of which emerges over a flowing accompaniment so ripe that Rachmaninoff might have written it. Presented without orchestral commentary, the melody has a chaste beauty; remember as you listen that it's all being covered by one hand. But soon the orchestra joins tenderly, with the English horn singing the chief theme as the soloist plays arpeggios and runs. The chief thematic idea, here placed in its most lyrical incarnation in the work, is passed to the clarinets, then the bassoons, but soon the tone grows more agitated. In an unusual instruction, Ravel tells the performer play arpeggios "*sans pédale*"—without the sustaining pedal that connects and blurs the notes—and every pianist's much used, not-so-secret weapon. He also writes the expression mark "*spiccato*"—"separated"—an instruction almost always given to string players, telling them to bounce the bow across the strings to achieve a detached effect, so here Ravel gives an unusual but clear direction to make his point. Winds and strings repeat the main theme over and over in the background as the piano part spreads out, both in an anticipatory harmony.

The next section is a complex grouping of ideas, dominated by a fierce, motoric march that Stravinsky could have written. A choppy falling chord sequence given first by the trumpets, then the piano, then later the flutes is heard a number of times, adding commentary to the march. The keyboard also introduces an appoggiatura—a way of sliding one note into the next—that will play an important role at the end of the work. In spite of the force of the march, yet another figure, an unforgettably catchy, dance-like tune given in triplets (three notes in the space of two) emerges in the keyboard. This is the most energetic and memorable idea in the march section. There are also two short interruptions in the form of a playful, lighter textured, scherzolike passage dominated by the bright timbres of the flute, piccolo, and harp. The soloist accompanies in this section with a relatively easy series of arpeggios and runs. The march rhythm returns, but quietly, as, in one of the few comical moments in this serious and dramatic work, the bassoon enters on a long solo in a different rhythm from the march, and apparently oblivious to the prevailing rhythm. The soloist returns with the dancing triplets, but then a solo trombone picks up the bassoon's disconnected melody. In a complex development, the contest between the march-dance, the disconnected tune, tapping percussion, groaning strings, and sweeping scales for the woodwinds become locked a tense, intense, and strange struggle. Ravel breaks it off unexpectedly with a short repeat of the scherzolike passage.

Piano and strings pick out choppy figuration in a new, tighter beat; this leads into a grandiose statement of the main theme, interspersed with dramatic flourishes for the soloist. The stiff rhythm of the orchestral accompaniment is somewhat reminiscent of the *Boléro*. This culminates in a huge climax, followed by falling, anticipatory figuration for the strings and woodwinds. What's coming is a long, murderously difficult, but thematically tight cadenza for the piano.

This incredible three-minute passage dominates and fulfills the concerto's melodic and dramatic potential. It opens with arpeggios and runs from which thematic elements gradually emerge, even as what would be the left hand if the player were using both has to jump between notes at the very bottom of the keyboard and melodic material, in addition to ever-quickening runs higher up. Among these are the lyrical theme and the concerto's dominating idea, which emerges transfigured into a more open rhythm. Finally, strings and low woodwinds steal in quietly. The chief idea returns majestically compressed, but even more exciting is the appearance of the appogiaturas, here transformed by the brass into three shattering flashes of orchestral lightning, conveying an unmistakable ecstasy. With an unerring dramatic instinct, Ravel cuts off the vision, bringing back the march and the choppy falling figure, and ending the work in a powerful, thrillingly compressed, five-second-long micro-coda.

Piano Concerto in G Major

Certainly, there's more of dry, bright, sometimes hard sound the composer favored in the latter part of his career to be heard in the G Major Concerto, but that's not his only tonal strategy in this charming but subtle work. The second movement, for example, is sweetly and delicately scored. The multithemed opening movement also undermines the theory that the composer's inventive capacity diminished later in his career. In this concerto, Ravel specifies his orchestral forces carefully, thinning the woodwind section and even numbering the strings he wants: eight each for the first and second violins, six each in the viola and cello sections, and four double basses. Typical for Ravel, seven percussion instruments are specified, but he notes that two players can cover them all. While too big to be described as a chamber orchestra, it's obvious that the lush and plush timbre of a full symphony orchestra is not what he wanted.

Nothing demonstrates the differences in the personalities of the two concertos more clearly than their opening passages. In place of the mystery and darkness that informs the *Concerto pour la main gauche*, the first movement of the Concerto in G Major (CD Track 3) opens briskly with a crack in the percussion followed by some of the brightest sounds in the orchestra. And unlike the work for one hand, where the soloist isn't heard from until a few minutes in, here the piano is there from the start. The piano plays dizzy triplets that accompany the first of the movement's many themes, a bright and bouncy idea set to a sharp short-short-long rhythm and introduced by the piccolo, immediately taken up by the trumpet. A forceful statement of the short-short-long idea in full harmony followed closely by a powerful rising scale for the bassoons and brass show this as a work not just of brilliance, but of substance as well. There's a resemblance to Stravinsky's *Petrushka* in the bright sounds and to that work's well-known *Danse russe*—"Russian Dance"—in its rhythm, but these are momentary.

Once the orchestra has quieted down, the piano, left to its own ways, slows the tempo and plays an important, languid theme, to which a long-limbed, gracefully descending, blues-inspired figure is appended, then a thoughtful tune for the keyboard set over a limping rhythm, these three very different phrases forming a thematic unit. They're traded back and forth for a while, reaching a fully lyrical interlude, a relaxed phase of this sometimes hectic movement. But harps and brass lead into a new section, commanded by a driving perpetual motion for the piano. Here, busy passagework supports hints of the opening theme, which soon comes back, tailed by the blues phrase. A long, fierce scale for the soloist leads to a restatement of the opening idea, which, however, peters out quickly, giving way to the languid idea followed by an elaborate riff for the piano on the falling blues theme. In an unusual procedure, Ravel slows down and quiets almost all the players to allow the harp a gentle, unhurried restatement of the thoughtful melody. The full orchestra gives the blues theme its most striking incarnation, including strange trilled notes for the flute, clarinet, and trumpet, as the soloist spreads out grandly in triplets alongside. Scales in the woodwinds accompany a slow rendition of the thoughtful theme by the horn.

The trill-laden cadenza for the piano into which this leads, also based on the thoughtful tune, moves gradually into busier passagework for the soloist, which breaks into a powerfully motoric passage that includes the unusual appearance of the lowest note on the keyboard, which is struck twenty-four times in just a few seconds. A long buildup is developed by Ravel into a compressed return by the forceful version of the opening idea, here taken by the keyboard, and woodwinds and trumpets that chatter away more cheerfully. A brilliant moment where the G major chord is hammered out by the soloist and orchestra leads to a potent eight-chord falling sequence and a playful but sharp landing on the last one.

Being a work of contrast, the concerto's slow movement serves as its warm heart, set between more raucous companions. Taking Mozart as his inspiration, Ravel conceives a ruminative melody of great length—thirty-two measures that take about three minutes to play—and expansive lyricism. Presented by the solo instrument, the long, irregular tune also hints at another inspiration, that of Chopin,[2] whose *Berceuse*, Op. 57, presents a comparable melodic profile, which that composer subjects to ever more lavish ornamentation. Chopin sets his lullaby over an unchanging accompaniment during the course of the work's five or six minutes, whereas Ravel's left hand offers some variation. The melody is interesting, too, for the way it develops out of short phrases that turn into one long idea. As you get to know it, you'll find that the melody transforms itself from an assembled sequence into a single breath. Set in the center of the keyboard, the long tune unspools easily over the gentle rocking of the left hand, reaching a very mild climax, moments before the some orchestral companions, in pastel tones, steal in. These include the flute, singing high in its range, then the English horn, bassoons, and horns.

As the winds sigh out a rising figure, the piano begins a new role as accompanist, spinning out sixteenth-notes alongside fragments of the melody, now shared among woodwinds and strings. The movement reaches its most intense moments as the composer raises the volume a bit and asks the performer to play shorter notes, but this moment is so unemphatic and over so quickly that it can hardly be called a climax. The piano accompanies the English horn as it spins out the tune at length. There's a magical shift in harmony as the melody passes among the winds, before fragmenting gently under a long trill and rocking for the player's left hand.

Some critics find the finale to be on a lower plane than the first two movements, derivative of Stravinsky and Gershwin, whom Ravel met during his American visit.[3] While such influences might be perceived, the finale makes a good ending for the concerto, contrasting absolutely with the quietly lyrical slow movement while recalling the first movement's wilder moments. Compressed into a fast-moving, action-packed four minutes, Ravel's seems to fit well within traditional forms and styles for concerto finales; listen and make up your own mind.

Four loud, dry chords and a thump on the drums open a frantic, furious sequence for the soloist, set at "presto," one of the quickest tempo indications. A screeching clarinet, trombone, and piccolo add sliding, leaping, and tumbling commentary that flash by like coloristic effects, but are actually thematic. Pizzicato strings and giddy winds accompany a more cheerful dance-hall passage marked by difficult repeated note phrases. With a crack on the rute (a percussion instrument that's basically a bundle of sticks) the composer takes us off to the races as galloping figures for the horns and trumpets, trailed by keyboard, winds, and percussion chase one another amusingly; a marchlike phrase sounds more earnest. Quietly scurrying bassoons lead to a new phase, where all the elements are put into chase in ever-increasing volume. An astonishingly dissonant phrase for the piano turns out to be an incarnation of the racing horn calls. Now, except for one relatively calm interlude lasting a few seconds, the contest dashes ahead with ever-more-frenzied thematic compression and good humor. Squealing winds echo a tightly spinning phrase for the keyboard, ending the piece (as you might expect) on the four hard chords and the thump that kicked the movement off.

6 The Chamber Music

Chamber music is the fussy and discouraging term for a wide range of compositions for small instrumental ensembles of from two to eight or nine performers; it's also one of the noblest categories in music. The rubric reaches back five centuries or so to when music was classified by whether it was to be played in church or a secular setting, with the latter eventually becoming "chamber." The grouping contains some of the best music of all, by Ravel and just about every other important composer who wrote instrumental works and some who didn't, as well: even the operatic titan Verdi wrote an excellent string quartet.

Combinations of strings and keyboards dominate the duets, and the trios, too, which from the late eighteenth century have been ruled by the piano trio, for violin, cello, and, of course, the keyboard instrument. The string quartet, consisting of two violins, viola, and cello, is by far the most significant of the four-instrument groupings, as well as the most important category within chamber music. The string quartets of Haydn, who invented the form, Mozart, Beethoven, Schubert, Bartók, Britten, and others stand as supreme achievements. Above four instruments are ensembles for countless variations for strings, winds, and keyboard.

Ravel's works for chamber ensemble, few but crucial, fall into two groups, and span his whole career. The first is of big works, all one-offs, mostly in set forms. There's a late and brilliant sonata for piano and violin. There is one string quartet, and a piano trio, both well known and loved, which stand among the top examples of their respective forms. A duet sonata for violin and cello from the composer's maturity is also of high quality but, due to its lean textures, harder to approach. And the Introduction and Allegro for Harp, Flute, Clarinet, and String Quartet is a marvelous work for seven-instrument ensemble. Then, there are three smaller items for violin and piano. Although formally less ambitious, these works, the most famous of which is the *Tzigane*, all show Ravel's high craftsmanship.

String Quartet in F Major

Ravel composed his single contribution to the quartet literature in 1902 and 1903. This landmark of his early development comes about a decade after Debussy's quartet, which is the latter's only work in the form as well. Invariably joined in music lovers' minds, the two quartets have a natural affinity, partly because the composers are the twin French giants of the same era, and partly because of the characters of the works, which are actually quite distinct. Debussy's quartet, muscular and powerful, is an atypical display of strict formal structure for a creator who generally liked to let works find their own shapes. Debussy cast his quartet in cyclical form, which means that one theme in various guises dominates all four movements and returns triumphantly at the end. Ravel pays homage to Debussy by bringing back material from the first section in the third, lending his quartet a cyclical feel, if not full-out pursuit of the procedure. Also like Debussy, Ravel also employs plucked (pizzicato) sonority to dominate his second movement. But where Debussy's is pithy and fierce, Ravel's quartet is driven by a potent and unflagging lyrical impulse. And, although Ravel's brilliant finale surges on rhythmic motion and the fascination imparted by the unusual beat in which most of it is cast, it, too, is filled with melody. In his quartet, beauty, balance, and high technique are constant, making the work a significant and beloved contribution to the genre.

The melodious first movement is organized in what's known as sonata form, meaning that it's set in three big sections and a shorter concluding one. In the opening part (known as the exposition), three melodies, each more gorgeous than the last, are set forth. The tranquil opening idea, over a calm rising line for the second violin and cello, and into which Ravel builds a little echo, establishes the work's dominant mood. The second theme, sung by the first violin over a rustling accompaniment, shows more animation as the ensemble pass its swaying phrases around. A busy transitional passage leads into the third idea, yet another ecstatic tune, related to the opening melody but into which the composer adds triplets, the pulsing rhythmic device that squeezes three notes into the space of two. Into this already rich mix the composer introduces a hovering fourth idea, sung by the viola and cello to shimmering accompaniment by the violins.

In the second section of the sonata form (the development), the themes are broken apart and subjected to passionate and fantastical mixing, reaching a moment of ecstasy on the rhythm of the opening phrase over surging figuration for the second violin and cello. In this wonderful passage Ravel takes full advantage of the wide range of sound string instruments can produce. In the third section (the recapitulation), the opening material is presented again, albeit slightly altered and amplified, and thrown into different light as well for their transformations in the development. There's a short closing section (the coda) where Ravel slows down, allowing us to admire the beauty of the ideas one last time.

Ravel pays his most open homage to Debussy's quartet in the quick second movement, the scherzo, both set chiefly to the pleasing sound of plucked instruments (CD Track 4). Ravel's movement, more fleet-footed and lyrical than Debussy's, opens with a pizzicato tune of lightly Javanese flavor. In the high age of orientalism in western music, Ravel's restraint keeps such coloring well in hand, preventing the material from cloying. The pizzicato phrases give way to what is probably the best tune in this melody-rich work, pulsing, mysterious, and ecstatic, sung by the first violin, the composer's marking that it be "*bien chanté*"—"sung out." The trio—the slow middle part of the movement—consists of a melody played by the cello high its range, a languid waltzlike phrase, then a fragment of the movement's great tune, leading finally to the pizzicato opening passage where the composer again shows off his rhythmic mastery.

In the slow third movement, Ravel combines new material, in the form of an expressive tune for the violin, with recollections, the initial one marked "*très calme*," of the first movement's tranquil opening melody. Its middle section, introduced by a declaimed phrase for the cello, moves at a more flowing pace, and continues to be dominated by the cello, which soars in a hovering melody over arpeggios for the first violin and viola, which eventually share the tune. Several times again, though, Ravel brings back the first movement's opening idea, always as though a remote memory, an effect he achieves by placing it in distant harmonies. In the last of these, a falling figure that opened the movement joins the recollection, which by now has assumed mottolike significance and with which the composer ends the section.

The more dramatic finale is cut from a different mold, as Ravel deploys unusual five-beat meters, rather than two-, three-, or four-beat bars we're used to. This is the technical explanation for what you'll experience as a sense of being a bit off balance or breathless, which, however, also acts to pull the material forward. After the agitated opening statements, the composer is profligate with melody, as before; yet he keeps to his habitual delicacy. Further broadening the work's already wide sonic range, he employs harmonics, where the players touch the strings lightly, producing a hollow whistling tone, as part of the accompaniment for one of the movement's big melodies. The closing passage is a climactic restatement of the rushing opening measures, punctuated by big plucked chords for the viola and cello, providing a cathartic ending for this wonderful work.

Introduction and Allegro for Harp, Flute, Clarinet, and String Quartet

Ravel gave first billing to the instrument that dominates this work, which one commentator helpfully calls "a miniature harp concerto rather than a septet."[1] Although only ten minutes long, this 1905 composition is spacious and satisfying. Again, both Ravel and Debussy wrote similar, contemporaneous works, with Debussy's *Danses sacrée et profane*—"Sacred and Profane Dances"—for harp and strings (no winds) dating from the year before. As with their string quartets, Debussy's dances are stranger and denser than Ravel's airy masterwork.

Opening in a slow tempo with an arching phrase, the introduction begins the procession of the dance-like themes that form the piece. Ravel builds anticipation with gently accelerating tempos, thicker textures, and more fully formed melodic ideas. The introduction and allegro are neatly joined, the harp presents the handsome first subject alone, with the rest of the ensemble then adding its commentary. A second idea of a mysterious and mystical cast is played by the winds with punctuation by the harp; there's a surprising return of the material of the introduction. The harp plays the second theme, which turns out to be the climactic one, in a thick, almost pianistic phrase; the ensemble reinterprets it with growing intensity. Finally, the harpist plays a long and elaborate cadenza—a virtuosic passage designed to show off the soloist's skill—in which the work's many themes are reverently reviewed. Finally the ensemble rejoins quietly but in high excitement, as Ravel recapitulates, then begins the long, quick-tempo coda, where themes find exciting new rhythmic incarnations as the music reaches unmistakable ecstasy before the final, rushing phrase.

Trio for Piano, Violin, and Cello in A Minor

Like the string quartet, the piano trio is an important category, filled with noble works by Haydn, Mozart, Beethoven, Schubert, Mendelssohn, Brahms, Dvořák, Tchaikovsky, and Shostakovich. But even in heavyweight company like this, Ravel's Piano Trio of 1914 stands as a landmark. Along with *Daphnis et Chloé* it's perhaps the climax of the composer's rich prewar style, it's a big piece, filled with ideas that are worked out rigorously but lavishly. All three instrumental parts are elaborate, complex, and very difficult to play, so only three virtuosos will be up to its challenges.

A delicate chant with an irresistible dancelike underpinning stated by the piano, the gentle pulse of the left hand animating the questioning theme played in the right, opens the trio (CD Track 5); it's also one of Ravel's most inspired ideas. The keyboard adds decoration that soon grows agitated as the now pulsating theme is worked through elaborate and difficult figuration for all three instruments. The hovering second theme enters, sounded by the strings over gentle chords for the keyboard. You'll know the development has begun when you hear the rhythm of the first theme deep in the piano's bass register. Here, Ravel heats things up furiously with embroidery that's elaborate but always controlled; the peaceful second theme returns, bringing motion to a near halt. There's no recapitulation, but instead a long, continually slowing coda in which both themes are recalled, with the first heard last, as though from an immense distance.

The title of the second movement, *Pantoum*, refers to a Malaysian poem, the delicate rhythm of which Ravel mimics in this remarkable scherzo, easy for listeners to like but challenging to execute. As in the parallel movement of the String Quartet, the orientalism of the sparkling opening theme is light handed and charming, and although Ravel keeps to one beat, he introduces rhythmic complications as well as hair-trigger shifts in touch from bowed to pizzicato to harmonics for the violin. The composer builds the second portion of the theme, marked by triplets, to a swift, impassioned climax. He cools down for the middle section, set for gorgeous, choralelike chords for the piano beneath continued busy activity for the strings. Rhythmic complexities reach a high point as strings and keyboard move in contrasting time signatures (4/2 and 3/4, respectively). The movement ends, as is typical for a three-part scherzo, on a return to the opening material.

Passacaille, the title for the slow third movement, is a type of variation based on a short theme form that reached its height in the baroque era. It's probably better known as by its Italian name, passacaglia. Typically those by Bach, Handel, and others are grand or stern in character; Ravel's has some of those affects, but in the context of this wild and passionate work, the third-movement *passacaille* serves primarily as an island of calm. The tranquil theme stated deep in the left hand of the piano never leaves the stage through the course of the ten variations that it engenders. Most are calm, though some, including the majestic fourth, the slippery, chromatic fifth, and the heroic sixth, present thicker textures, are louder, and reach for ecstasy. Those that follow are quiet and thinner, until the closing phrase, which mirrors the opening in feeling, if not in precise detail.

The finale, which begins without pause, is set, like that of the String Quartet, in unusual bars of five and seven beats, again lending a sense that one is off balance. The opening theme is lyrical and may remind you of the first movement's meditative opening subject, but here Ravel always rushes ahead passionately. The second theme, built of massive chords for the piano decorated by wild trills for the violin and cello, is ecstatic, and very difficult to play. Climactic by nature, this is the theme that Ravel builds to a sonority that's remarkable for three instruments, striking past the borders of chamber music toward the orchestral. Listen for the warlike mock-trumpet calls for the piano, followed by a swift lyrical interlude, before the climax of the chordal theme and the triumphant rhetoric of the coda.

Sonata for Violin and Cello

Completed in 1922 and dedicated *À la mémoire de Claude Debussy*, this will be the hardest of Ravel's works for chamber ensemble—and perhaps of his entire oeuvre—for the first-time listener to like or appreciate. Its difficulty is twofold: first, the sound of the two string instruments, not softened by piano or wind, are tough going; second, by the 1920s the composer's leaner, more dissonant style makes the sonata a spiky earful. The energy of the scherzo and the wit of the finale offer the most immediate paths into this challenging but significant and beautiful music. If you've heard the pieces for solo violin and cello by Johann Sebastian Bach, you'll have an idea of how much a great composer can make of limited means, which is just what Ravel does here, as well.

The first movement consists of contrasting thematic ideas, one flowing, the other more choreographic, which Ravel juxtaposes in a sonata debate. As in the String Quartet, he deploys the wide range of sound strings can produce, including pizzicato and harmonics. Although tight and linear, the music can become pleasing once you give the composer's focused method room to work its way into your imagination. The driving second movement may remind you of Stravinsky, of Bartók, or of another Hungarian composer, Zoltán Kodály, in its rough energy, uncharacteristic of Ravel, and rhythmic sophistication, as the instruments hammer at each other with startling fury. Surely the composer's ferocity is tinged with irony as he uses only eight strings to create it. Here, as throughout the sonata, pizzicato remains a key coloristic element, as are harmonics, trills, and glissandi, a sliding effect, a notable example of which for the cello ends the movement.

A solemn but tender theme for the cello opens the slow movement, the climax of which is a dissonant middle section that still sounds strikingly modern. In the third section of this three-part movement, the violin takes up the opening theme, first deep in its range, then soaring up with a phrase in a bold harmony banned in compositional textbooks. The finale is probably the most fun to hear of the four movements, but its playfulness masks a fantastic complexity, as the players have to change the beat and their bowing continually during the bouncy opening phrases. Ravel introduces fiddly, folklike elements and more violent moments that recall the scherzo. Once again, his coloristic range is wide, and he ends in a percussive uproar for its two instruments. You can pat yourself on the back if this difficult and daring music speaks to you.

Sonata for Violin and Piano in G Major

Ahead of this familiar late composition is a one-movement sonata from 1897 that Ravel never published, that came to light thirty years after his death. Known as the "Posthumous Sonata," this student work, written when the composer was twenty-two, is a meandering, polished, slightly neutral piece that will not disappoint if you keep your expectations moderate. Its chief interest lies in the hovering opening theme, which, as commentators have pointed out,[2] anticipates that of the first movement of the Piano Trio. Aside from the instrumental pairing, though, it has little in common with the brilliant late-period sonata that cost Ravel so much effort over the four frequently interrupted years it took to complete.

Curiously, Ravel had come to consider the two instruments essentially incompatible, so, particularly in the first movement he keeps them apart, often to startling effect. Here, the rich instrumental writing of the trio is nowhere to be found. Ironic, dry, elegantly austere, wiry, witty, and even funny at times, this work shows the composer's late style at its most highly evolved. The opening movement, in sonata form, starts with a lilting, disembodied melody for the piano, which the violin joins. The piano then shifts to commentary that sounds almost irrelevant, including a chicken-scratch figure that recurs often. The violin part swells into a big tune, which comes back later, and at even greater length. Beneath this Ravel thins the keyboard texture severely to handfuls of spare chords and dissonant gestures. As the material is recapitulated, the violin's long tune is brought back in a breathtaking incarnation as the piano chatters away quite independently. The contrapuntally inflected coda contrasts the lilting motion of the movement's opening phrase, here on the keyboard, beneath long-held, remote notes for the violin.

The charming second movement, titled *Blues*, will fool no one familiar with the real item, as it's a very French amalgam of about a third each of blues, jazz, and something entirely different. Ravel does deploy throughout the harmonic interval that's the thumbprint of the blues, but the chugging of the fiddle as it imitates a guitar, then slides like a saxophone or trombone, has too much artifice to suggest authenticity to American listeners. None of this ought to keep you from enjoying this witty specimen of tone painting, which later turns rather fierce as the fiddler plucks big chords and as the piano chews on a jazzy, skipping figure below. The composer will work blues inflections more subtly and effectively into the first movement of his Piano Concerto of 1931.

Another scratching figure kicks off the quick, brilliant finale in perpetual motion; from the fifteenth bar to the end, the violin never ceases its steady, furious stream of notes as the piano tries to keep up. The keyboard material is limited to a few figures: scurrying triplets and a short-short-long-long phrase trailed by a skipping figure. But the composer brings what sounds mechanical to a climax that's manic, funny, and ultimately joyful with these thematic scraps, as the supposedly incompatible pair reaches together for grandeur in the wild closing bars.

Smaller Works for Piano and Violin

There are three additional chamber pieces: the *Tzigane*, a Gypsy-inspired rhapsody of 1924 that is by far the best known; a *Habanera*; and the gentle *Berceuse sur le nom de Gabriel Fauré*—"Lullaby on the Name of Gabriel Fauré." *Tzigane*, whose title means "Gypsy," is one of Ravel's most familiar works, but in several ways a poor fit in this chapter on chamber music. It's here because it began life as a work for violin and piano, though it's equally well known in the orchestrated version. But its deliberately coarse affect takes *Tzigane* far from the intimate manner typical of chamber music; and, at ten minutes' playing time, it's hardly small. But it's a great work, not only as a showpiece for violin virtuosos, but as a display of Ravel's technique and of the layered ironies of his treatment of a familiar—not to say hackneyed—idea.

As we've seen, exotic influences formed an important current in European music from the mid-nineteenth century, with "Hungarian"—actually Gypsy flavored—a favorite. Seeking to sound wild, Liszt in his *Hungarian Rhapsodies* for piano is coarse—fun, but coarse. On the other side of the spectrum, the elegant *Hungarian Dances* of Brahms, and the *Slavonic Dances* of Dvořák are *soigné*, impeccably turned out. In *Tzigane*, Ravel contrives to seem wild and vulgar while actually writing impeccably, in his most characteristic way. That's because every detail of these remarkable scores, in both piano and orchestral versions, is thought through and worked out, with no effect thrown away. Its closest relative in Ravel's oeuvre may the *La Valse*, also powerfully ironic.

In case you're listening for the first time, the difficulty of the solo violin part is obvious, but it's even harder than it sounds, with frequent shifts of touch, timbre, speed, and dynamics (volume). Ravel asks the soloist to toss away, as though casually, long phrases of two notes at a time, and to make hair-trigger shifts between notes that bite deeply into the strings to scampering pizzicati, then back. *Tzigane* is daring harmonically, too, with dizzying shifts from its nominal keys that are rapid and frequent, many bitter dissonances coloring to the piece from beginning to end.

Putting all these considerations aside, *Tzigane* is popular because it's exciting and fun to listen to. Its form is in straightforward imitation of Liszt's *Hungarian Rhapsodies*, with two big sections, the opening slow, moody, and passionate (or mock-passionate) the second quick, choreographic, then accelerating to a conventionally "driving" ending. If there's a cliché to use, Ravel uses it, taking each to its technical and expressive limits. The piano (or the harp in the orchestral version) imitates the cimbalom, a dulcimer-like Hungarian instrument played with hammers, copied frequently by Liszt. *Tzigane* opens with a slow, murderously difficult solo passage where the violin weeps, moans, and swaggers in uncanny imitation of the Gypsy manner, occupying well over a third of the work's playing time. The main theme of the next part is introduced in a brooding incarnation. The second part begins over cimbalom-like arpeggios, introducing and exploring the main theme in a more open, swinging gait, though swooning figuration returns, too. Finally, a gurgling quick-tempo dance enters, which, along with the main theme, carries the work to its apparently furious end. So convincing is Ravel's mimesis that even after getting to know the work, it's difficult to believe that every effect, down to the last smeared harmony and rhythmic jolt, is written in the score. Our enjoyment of *Tzigane* may feel almost like a guilty pleasure: never forget that in it the composer is playing brilliantly on our expectations for Gypsy music.

The smoky *Habanera* for violin and piano is one of three versions of an 1897 work that effectively displays early but potent pull of Spanish music on the master. There are no surprises here, as the violin carries an evocative tune over a straightforward rhythmic base for the keyboard. The other versions are for two pianos and full orchestra, as the third movement of the *Rapsodie espagnole*.

Short and gentle, the two-minute *Berceuse* is a tribute to Fauré (still living at the time of its composition in 1922), who taught Ravel, then stood behind him in his wars with the Conservatoire. Ravel invented a melody based on notes whose names are included in "Gabriel Fauré": G, A, B, and so forth. So, although the piece sounds simple, it's actually quite polished. Simplicity is suggested in the rocking motion of the piano accompaniment, and the violin plays muted throughout.

7 The Orchestral Works

With only one exception, Ravel's large-scale orchestral works were originally conceived as ballets. As we've seen, this pattern is entirely typical for this crossover specialist and constant re-creator of his own work, a trait requiring continual reminders and explanations. We looked at the transcriptions of works for piano in chapter 4; here we'll examine the orchestral pieces usually grouped as straight orchestral music. But even that isn't really accurate, as one of the *Rapsodie espagnole*'s four movements is a transcription of a work originally for piano, and, as we've seen, *Ma Mère l'Oye* began life as a composition for four-hand piano. In the end, none of these conditions matter. I'll explain them, but the music is in every case extraordinary, and that's all you'll need to focus on.

Ravel's career as an orchestral composer began in his student years, from which an overture to *Shéhérazade* from 1898 has survived. The work has been recorded and can be heard on YouTube or MP3. The material itself, typical orientalist fantasy of the day, has a bit less character than what the master would later devise, but *Shéhérazade* is a tasty work that shows the composer's skills already highly evolved at age twenty-three. His writing for woodwinds and percussion is already fine, calling with the latter for an unusually large and sophisticated section. There's only the most tenuous relationship—mostly of mood and instrumental coloring—between the overture and the great song cycle of 1903 of the same name, but the overture is of real merit and well worth hearing. By five years later, Ravel refined and strengthened his thematic material, as well as his orchestral technique, already at a high level. Quite simply, he was one of the greatest masters of orchestral color, his gifts setting him apart in an era of great orchestrators.

In none of his orchestral works does Ravel follow symphonic sonata form: everything is given over to the pursuit of the exotic and the colors that flow from its various streams, from Asian to Spanish to fairy tale to Greek myth. Even in *La Valse* (1920), where he stays closer to the more standard European model of a Viennese waltz, the work is steered by its orchestral color, which Ravel manipulates with his usual skill. As we'll see, the shadowy nature and cataclysmic ending of *La Valse* calls for a more dark-hued treatment for orchestra. In his first fully orchestral work of his maturity, the *Rapsodie espagnole* of 1908, his mastery stands as some of the most sophisticated yet clear ever conceived. With the ballet *Daphnis et Chloé*, the composer reaches a pinnacle where he keeps the lucidity that's one of his hallmarks but with a rare sumptuousness. For Ravel, *Daphnis* represented a peak he neither needed nor attempted to surpass. In the *Boléro*, his final orchestral piece, we may even hear a further expression of the focus of *La Valse*, fitting for this thematically severe exercise.

Rapsodie espagnole

Ravel completed this symphonic evocation of Spain in 1908, although the third-movement *Habanera* was written in 1895 as a work for two pianos. He added it to this four-movement composition, where, obviously, it fits quite well. Interestingly, the score shows the date of composition in parentheses at the head of that movement only. He inserted it because he was accused of copying Debussy in his Spanish mode, and wanted to show that he had been there first.[1] Debussy's great tone poem *Ibéria* and Ravel's *Rapsodie* are contemporaneous, with *Ibéria* premiering in 1910. Both are important and fine examples of their composers' respective skills, as well as of the sway that exotic elements held over European music in the late nineteenth and early twentieth centuries. As we've seen, the two composers maintained a distance that was respectful, at least on Ravel's part; their composing symphonic suites on Spanish themes at more or less the same time is coincidental, and nothing more, only a reflection of the power of the exotic in music, and of Spain on the imagination of French composers of the day. Of course, you'll want to get to know, then will respect, enjoy, and appreciate both, as they're equally fine and steeped in the idiom, and to compare two Spanish tone poems by the two greatest French composers of the era is too tempting to resist. For example, while not to knock *Ibéria*, Ravel's stunning originality as an orchestrator is on full display in the *Rapsodie espagnole*. Although he applies Spanish flavoring heavily throughout the *Rapsodie espagnole*, it's anything but a lightweight musical travelogue, with all four of its movements shadowed by mystery, strangeness, and menace. Immediate predecessors of both include the familiar orchestral suite *España* by Chabrier, the rather less known *Capriccio espagnol* of Rimsky-Korsakov, and looming over both, Bizet's *Carmen*. A more remote ancestor is Liszt's clattery *Rhapsodie espagnole* for piano.

One of Debussy's more cheerful works, *Ibéria* opens with a grand, choreographic gesture. But Ravel opts for a smoky nocturne to set a mood of mystery and to stimulate our anticipation in an entirely different way. The *Prélude à la nuit*—"Prelude to the Night"—that stands as the first section of the *Rapsodie espagnole* is dominated by a four-note falling figure that hardly leaves the scene and acts as a hypnotic background for other figuration. (The four-note motive also reappears in the second and fourth parts.) The one glamorous sighing phrase for the violins that appears midway through carries a great deal of weight, as here and throughout the *Rapsodie* Ravel withholds from his listeners big tunes, with one notable exception in the final section. Instead of writing fully formed melodies, he allows melodic phrases to rise up out of the Spanish rhythms and orchestral colors, particularly that of the percussion. And in the *Prélude à la nuit*, the falling four-note figure provides a steady background for instrumental effects that are mostly gentle and suggestive, and perhaps as close as the composer gets to impressionism.

There are two elaborate cadenzas—showy passages—for woodwinds, the first for the clarinets, and the second for the bassoons that suggest birdcalls, for which the falling figure pauses momentarily. Ravel's instrumentation is magical, with minimal participation by the brass, and a crucial contribution by the celesta (a keyboard instrument with a tinkling but piercing sound that's best known for its appearance in the "Dance of the Sugarplum Fairy" in Tchaikovsky's *Nutcracker*), which takes up the falling figure toward the end. To strengthen the hazy, nocturnal atmosphere, strings and horns often play muted. *Les Parfums de la nuit*—"Scents of the Night"—the central movement of *Ibéria*, takes a similar approach, with an atmospheric opening and the fade-outs of its closing pages, but Debussy cuts loose with several ripe melodies in the middle. Instrumental strategies are similar, too, with woodwinds deployed to suggest insect noises. Like Ravel, Debussy also finds a role for the celesta.

The brief *Malagueña* that follows opens with deep-toned rhythmic figures from which flowing phrases for winds, then the violins, emerge. The trumpets enter with a bright, brittle tune that's as much rhythm as melody, but it's interrupted by a slower, moodier sequence. Again textures thicken and tempos increase, but a long-spun recitative-like melody for the English horn in its nasal high register, melancholy, appears, soon backed by the falling four-note figure that dominated the first movement. A rising phrase for strings and gurgling winds ends this impression of the dance that says all it needs to in two minutes, but which satisfies with its polish and wit.

Like the *Malagueña*, the slow *Habanera* manages to appear easy and relaxed even though it's constructed with the utmost care. And, as in the nocturnal first movement, isolated phrases that carry the weight of melodies emerge above the steady, chugging pulse of the habanera (*long*-short-long-long). Ravel's writing for woodwinds, especially the clarinets, and percussion is worth your attention, as the tambourine, cymbal, snare, and bass drum join the timpani in a delicate grouping that shows the refinement of the composer's ear and technique while always sounding natural, and never aggressive or ostentatious. Like the *Prélude à la nuit*, the *Habanera* seems to fade cinematically into a smoky distance.

Feria—"Festival"—the fourth and last part of the *Rapsodie espagnole*, aligns interestingly alongside *Le Matin d'un jour de fête*—"A Festival Morning"—the final movement of *Ibéria*. But where Debussy paints a joyous and at times comic scene, Ravel's vision—a precursor of *La Valse*, as we'll see—is far more shadowy and ambiguous; each is utterly persuasive in its way.

Ravel opens his tone poem with a delicate cantering figure for flutes and harps that raises expectations. But almost immediately, chords played by the low winds and brass darken the picture. Muted trumpets echoed by the xylophone chatter a familiar "Spanish" rhythmic figure, and in a few moments the scene of the festival opens with the orchestra roaring the rhythm in full splendor as a broader phrase played by low strings and woodwinds takes center stage thematically. The flutes take up a curling arabesque, again of deeply Spanish flavor, which the other winds and the trumpets then join, seeming to round out the themes in a satisfying way: we feel as though we've walked from a dark side street into the bright square where the festival is being held. This opening prefigures that of *La Valse*, where, eleven years later, Ravel has us approach the ballroom as from outside, with fragments of dances sifting through an aural murk, then coming together by gradually rising volume and the iteration of full phrases.

Once these bright and cheerful elements have found their way to a thunderous climax, the composer thins the orchestral texture and slows the tempo radically. Over a delicately scored accompaniment, the English horn takes up a long, slow, slightly exaggerated lament that suggests flamenco, which a solo clarinet takes up and extends considerably; this by far the longest tune in the *Rapsodie*. Ravel's instrumental writing here is remarkably refined, and worth getting to know, such as where the harps and celesta join in high chords and the low brass make contributions that are gentle and never ponderous. In the middle of this, the harp and flute gently exhale the falling four-note figure from the first and second movements, which here seems ominous and disconcerting: we're forced to wonder what that obsessive nocturnal figure is doing here. But Ravel assigns it an important role, as it's taken up by the celesta's piercing tone.

Soon the grand phrases and rhythms return, but now underpinned by sweeping arpeggios for the harp and quick, unsettling harmonic shifts for the brass. The arabesque, which has the quality of a closing idea also comes back as if to suggest the approach of a happy ending, but again, Ravel fragments and distorts the thematic material, places slight but disturbing shifts into the harmony, a method he pursues to a very different, devastating conclusion in *La Valse*. Several menacing, oceanic glissandi—slides—for the strings and winds may unsettle you. And, although the bright, "Spanish" elements thunder away, Ravel inserts one last wild, wavelike glissando before the end, which seems as though it could just as easily send the material off the rails and into disaster, as he will with the eruptions that drive *La Valse* to its catastrophic end. Although the ending of the *Feria* is upbeat, Ravel has here developed the structure for the later tone poem's tragic closing.

Ma Mère l'Oye

Although somewhat less familiar than Ravel's other major orchestral works, *Ma Mère l'Oye*—"Mother Goose"—is one of the composer's most consistently fine compositions, a masterwork of his high middle period, deserving more appreciation and meriting close attention. In addition to the excellence of its material and astonishingly brilliant instrumentation, the five (or six, depending on which version) sections of *Ma Mère l'Oye* convincingly paint the wonders and terrors of the fairy tales recounted, with a sound and mood all its own.

Ravel worked on the score of *Ma Mère l'Oye* between 1908 and 1911. His original version, as a five-movement suite for four-hand piano, was to have been have been played by two young performers. The friends' daughters he hoped would play it eventually refused, so eventually he had to settle for young Conservatoire students. The composer then orchestrated the suite—the form in which it's most commonly heard—then revised the work into a full ballet, with his own scenario. For this, he added transitional passages that link the movements, as well as a whole new section, the *Danse du rouet*—"Dance of the Spinning Wheel"—all of which expand the work considerably. As we've seen, Ravel's orchestral transcriptions of piano works aren't necessarily better than the originals, just different approaches by a composer whose mastery of both keyboard and orchestral writing were prodigious. This certainly applies to *Ma Mère l'Oye*, where every version offers its own charm and appeal. And, although the suite is its most familiar incarnation, to be thorough I'll discuss the ballet, which is about ten minutes longer. Concision and compression are major qualities of the work in any of its forms, as Ravel says what he has to say eloquently, then moves on.

The *Prélude* depicts the remoteness of an imagined world with an unfailing sense of wonder. Woodwinds voice chords so slow as to suspend time, and soft calls for the muted horns aurally depict hunters in the far distance. But soon shimmering strings and the winds moving at a quicker pace hint eerily at magical events. The slow tempo returns, as the strings add weight and richness to the orchestral texture in a long, fervent phrase. Then Ravel repeats, although not literally, the quiet opening with its horn calls and the quicker, magical music for the full orchestra, which leads without pause into the *Danse du rouet* that he added to the original five-part work.

Trills from the strings carry the descriptive burden of the spinning wheel's sound, to which the gurgling of the winds adds an almost comical commentary. English speakers know this story as Sleeping Beauty, and the cheerful tone of the opening pages soon dissipates into flashing phrases that suggest menace and danger, as Sleeping Beauty pricks her finger, presumably at the strange, seesawing figures for the violins. Ravel brings back the opening phrase of the prelude, now suspended in remote harmonies.

The *Pavane de la Belle au bois dormant*—"Pavane for Sleeping Beauty"—the opening of the original version, opens with an extended, solemn melody for winds over plucked strings that's one of the composer's most sublime, striking a completely different, and timeless, note, purged of all preciousness or excess.

Moving gravely, the music combines grandeur, brooding passion, and remoteness in a manner that's pure and inimitable Ravel. He passes an echo of the melody briefly to the strings, before a shriek from the piccolo interrupts, breaking the mood, as does a swift but striking passage where all the strings produce a dense, clicking sound by playing *col legno*; that is, with the wooden sides of their bows. Even though less than three minutes long, slow, and quiet, you can expect to be haunted by this memorable passage.

The fairy tale that follows, *Les Entretiens de la Belle et de la Bête*—"The Dialogue of Beauty and the Beast"—feels more relaxed than what came before, but it's just as polished, making a particularly good example of Ravel's orchestral touch at its lightest. Three extracts from the story as retold by compiler of fairy tales Madame Leprince de Beaumont are set at the head of the section. In the first, Beauty compliments the Beast on his kindheartedness; in the second, the emboldened Beast proposes marriage, which Beauty gently declines. In the third extract, the Beast is transformed into a handsome prince, and Beauty accepts his proposal.

An easy waltz reminiscent of the music of Ravel's one-time friend, the minimalist-absurdist composer Erik Satie, is sung by the clarinet over a mild accompaniment for the strings. Lacking Ravel's technique, however, Satie always stays put thematically and harmonically, whereas Ravel shifts with the restlessness typical of more serious composers. In a most unusual strategy here, the contrabassoon, a harsh and weird sounding wind instrument that's rarely used for solos, depicts the Beast's grumbling voice. A compressed and intensified version of the waltz depicts the warmth of Beauty's replies. And a simple glissando—a slide—for the harp, followed by an ironically sentimental violin solo depict the Beast's magical transformation. A final, gentle iteration of the waltz ends the section.

The next section, *Petit Poucet*, is a setting of a Tom Thumb tale in which the child-size hero's clever scheme to use a trail of bread crumbs to mark his path through the forest is foiled by birds that feed on the crumbs. Ravel captures this legend with wandering figures in irregular rhythms for the muted violins, over which floats a plaintive melody for the oboe, which then passes to its deeper-pitched cousin, the English horn. The strings dominate a climax notable for the lonely longing expressed, as then with violins, piccolos, and flutes, Ravel imitates the screeches of the birds that have ruined Petit Poucet's plan. With a pithiness that's admirable and entirely typical for Ravel, these brilliantly executed phrases pass swiftly, and are not repeated. Petit Poucet's wandering melody returns, now more twilit, as this alarming tale depicted at a distance and with calm, ends on a rising, plaintive phrase for the oboe.

A dawnlike transition moves from the cool solemnity of the Petit Poucet's wanderings to the bright instrumental textures and high orientalism of the next dance, *Laideronnette, impératrice des pagodes*, which translates bewilderingly as "Little Ugly Girl, Empress of the Pagodas." As it's not essential to know the plot, let's just say that the little ugly girl is the heroine of the fairy tale *Serpentin vert*—"The Green Serpent"—and that *pagodas* refers to a Far Eastern musical instrument, a vertical array of bells called a pagoda, and not to temples. This dance, a great treat for the ear, also represents one of the composer's most orientalist moments. Ravel's light touch, swift motion—the music seems to fly—and orchestral skill makes his Asian-flavored music hold up better than that by many others.

Short, overlapping phrases that recall the open-sounding music of Java and Bali that made a strong impression on Ravel and others, and the bright sounds of the flute, harp, and celesta, then bright flashes for the percussion, introduce the chief melodic idea, a busy, cheerful, though slightly abstracted tune shared among oboe, flute, and English horn. Led by the clattering of an excited xylophone, a crescendo for the full orchestra paves the way for a broader processional theme intoned by the horns, punctuated by soft strokes on the gong, with the tune then passing to the clarinets for a gentler iteration. This gives way gradually to cooler phrasing and harmony, then a return of the busy main theme, again introduced by flashing percussion, and brightened further by the xylophone, harp, and celesta. Another crescendo led by the xylophone brings us to the final phrases, in bright, hard, dissonant harmony.

If my description makes the music sound excessively clattery or dated, then put the book down and listen. What you'll hear are Ravel's exquisite taste, his refusal to dawdle, and, of course, his matchless skill with the orchestra. *Laideronnette* is pure magic, and easy to enjoy.

A extended transitional passage, featuring the distant horn calls of the opening prelude, and the *col legno* clicking of the connecting passage after *Pavane de la Belle au bois dormant*, and a mockingly sweet violin solo lead into *Le Jardin féerique*—"The Fairy Garden"—the final section of *Ma Mère l'Oye*, where Ravel displays his gifts of refinement and restraint once more. The piece opens with a melody for the strings that's solemn, tender, and a bit remote, again in Ravel's most characteristic manner. It's developed richly and with no sense of hurry as the composer gradually introduces the rest of the orchestral groups, first the woodwinds, followed by the harp, celesta, horns, and finally the percussion. (Ravel doesn't use trumpets or trombones in *Ma Mère l'Oye*, their absence lightening and softening its orchestral textures.) The violin gets another solo, which the celesta underlines with some magical harmonic shifts; from here Ravel builds to a climax that's fervent and touching, to which the horns add repeated, chiming notes. The final measures are a triumphant apotheosis of and for the orchestra, underpinned by sweeping figures for the harp. Lasting about three and one-half minutes, and with material that's entirely comparable in melodic profile, emotional affect, and quality, this accomplishes most of what Mahler takes about twenty-five to do in the finale of his Third Symphony.

Daphnis et Chloé

Daphnis et Chloé is Ravel's composition on the largest scale, and it's generally considered to be his most important—his greatest—as well. Even though it's a ballet, choreographed performances are extremely rare: when performed complete, *Daphnis* is almost always heard as an hour-long symphonic work. And it's even more familiar when broken into one of two suites, usually the second, which contains its most famous and admired passage, the *Lever du jour*—"Daybreak"—as well as the exciting concluding section, often referred to as the *Bacchanale*. The elements now known as the Suite No. 1 were performed in April 1911, before the completion of the score the following year.

As you're acquainting yourself with *Daphnis*, you'll need to keep in mind that Ravel was composing a ballet score to a scenario—a story line—not a symphony or a tone poem, and that the music describes events onstage. It's essential to remember as well that the choreographic sense is strong throughout this, one of the greatest ballet scores ever written, an equal to Tchaikovsky's *Nutcracker* and Stravinsky's *Le Sacre du printemps* and *Petrushka*. Ravel does, however, unify *Daphnis* by means of thematic motives, tonality, and other devices; and unlike many ballets, it's not episodic but a work of unity and considerable momentum.

By then a well-established composer, Ravel was approached in 1909 by Sergei Diaghilev, the impresario of the Ballets Russes, the dance company that dominated the European stage in the early twentieth century. Its male star, Vaslav Nijinsky, was a high-wattage performer comparable in his athletic appeal to Rudolf Nureyev and Mikhail Baryshnikov decades later. The Ballets Russes (which never danced in Russia, by the way) was one of the most significant sources of musical commissions in the first quarter of the last century, with a staggering roster of masterpieces composed for it, including *Daphnis*, Debussy's *Jeux* ("Games," one of his greatest orchestral works), *El sombrero de tres picos*—"The Tricornered Hat"—by Manuel de Falla, and a string of scores by Stravinsky, including the two mentioned above, as well as *L'Oiseau de feu*—"The Firebird," *Pulcinella*, *Renard*, and *Apollon musagète*—"Apollo." Also showing the company's reach and prestige, Richard Strauss composed for it a setting of the Biblical story of Joseph, called the *Josephslegende*.

Diaghilev may have been a visionary producer, but he was erratic and difficult. In 1914, Ravel and Diaghilev had a very public dispute when the latter produced *Daphnis* several times without the chorus to save money, in response to which the composer complained angrily in the newspapers, with Diaghilev firing back.[2] Ravel's experiences (later with *La Valse*) left him disgusted and unwilling to deal with the Russian, and in fact the composer may even have challenged Diaghilev to a duel, though none ever took place. Without question Ravel refused in public to shake Diaghilev's hand at the 1925 premiere of *L'Enfant et les sortilèges*.[3] There was considerable turmoil during the rehearsals of the ballet. Most of the blow-ups involved Nijinsky, Diaghilev, and the choreographer Michel Fokine, but Ravel got his share of headaches, too. Conductor Pierre Monteux, a Ravel specialist over his long career, rehearsed the work carefully. Monteux commented, "All the musicians in the orchestra, and I might say in Paris, knew this was Maurice Ravel's greatest work. . . ."[4]

Set in the ancient Greece of legend, the ballet is in three parts, which are performed with momentary pauses between them; these are broken into shorter scenes and sections in which various dances and action take place. The first part consists of an introduction, followed by a solemn *Danse religieuse*, in which young shepherds and shepherdesses pay homage to three nymphs. Daphnis and Chloé enter, as lighthearted contests and mildly comic events take place, but later pirates attack, and carry off Chloé. Statues of the nymphs come to life, as the god Pan displays sympathy for Daphnis's plight. In the second part, Chloé tries to escape, but the pirates force her to dance. Suddenly strange sounds and sights, including the appearance of satyrs, Pan's emissaries, reveal the god's anger and frighten the pirates off. Part 3 opens with the musical depiction of daybreak that is the best-known passage in the score. Daphnis awakes, looking for Chloé, who returns. The couple dances a tribute to Pan, then the entire company joins in a wild dance of triumph.

Daphnis et Chloé is not only Ravel's most significant work, but one of the landmarks of twentieth-century music—indeed, of all music. In it, he sums up several musical currents: perhaps the highest tide in the history of ballet music; his sophisticated techniques and skill at creating polished aural surfaces; and the flexibility and opulence of the late-romantic orchestra. In an age of great ballet scores, *Daphnis* holds its own, while allowing the composer to speak in his distinct and mature voice. Unlike opera, nineteenth-century ballet music is typically bland, generic, and sometimes precious, allowing pretty performers to do pretty things onstage. The big personality of *Daphnis* shows Ravel's early appreciation and application of Stravinsky's contributions to the genre. Finally, *Daphnis* is one of the most complex scores ever written. We have to assume Manuel Rosenthal knew what he was saying when he commented that *L'Heure espagnole* was the most complex of Ravel's scores (see page 125), because *Daphnis* is so rich that it can only be a close second.

One aspect of Ravel's achievement in *Daphnis* demonstrates the international side of music, as discussions often overstate the supposed grip on composers of "national" schools and styles. My colleague David Hurwitz is correct in pointing out that skilled composers from all countries borrow and reinterpret ideas and techniques, as Mahler did in his Symphony No. 2 with motifs and affects borrowed from Beethoven, Wagner, and Verdi.[5] *Daphnis* shows Ravel making his closest approach to the orchestral virtuosity of his slightly older German contemporary Richard Strauss, whose instrumental techniques and strategies he admired, studied, and absorbed.[6] In terms of style, these two masters have more in common than many might think, as long as you're willing to put aside such generalizations as "French lightness" and "Germanic complexity." Before Ravel pared down his style after World War I, both composers favored complex but transparent orchestral textures, and both display a detached, ironic quality that seems to amplify the power and charm of Ravel's work, but at times makes Strauss sound slick. Additionally, it's possible that the closing dance—the *Bacchanale*—was inspired by music of Hector Berlioz, the singular French master of the nineteenth century.

Without question, *Daphnis et Chloé* is unthinkable without the sound of the late-romantic symphony orchestra, to which it is an outstanding homage in an era rich with tributes by Debussy, Richard Strauss, Stravinsky, Mahler, Berg, and others. Ravel's treatment of the orchestra and chorus in *Daphnis et Chloé* would make a study on its own, and is as integral to the work's greatness as the thematic material.

Even though *Daphnis* employs an enormous orchestra, the sound of the work is clean and lucid, except of course in those few moments when the composer deliberately seeks to achieve murky or boisterous effects. Ravel makes much (though of course not continual) use of mutes that dampen and reduce the sound of the brass and string instruments, giving the work a burnished sound, a sort of sonic matte finish. Again, the orchestration is so elaborate and brilliant that the only way to appreciate Ravel's achievement is to listen, with a score in hand, if at all possible. (This is a rewarding way to become familiar with a new piece, and not as hard as it may sound, even if you don't read music.)

The woodwinds, especially the flutes, have to perform unusual and virtuosic deeds, imitating Pan's and shepherd's pipes, birdsong, and a variety of other coloristic roles throughout the work. The longest, most virtuosic solo in the work is for the flute, a lyrical accompaniment to the pas de deux of Daphnis and Chloé in part 3 following their reuniting and preceding the final *Bacchanale.* The composer calls for an enlarged flute section consisting of four instruments. In addition to the standard two flutes and piccolo, there's the rare appearance of an alto flute, a longer instrument with a lower range and an insinuatingly throaty, cooing tone. Ravel keeps the alto flute busy throughout the work, even giving it a few short solos.

It's hard to think of another composition where the percussion section is as large and varied as what Ravel deploys in *Daphnis*, but is used with such subtlety and restraint. The score calls for fourteen percussion instruments, including the little hand cymbals known as crotales, triangle, tambourine, castanets, celesta, glockenspiel, and xylophone, in addition to the standard contingent of timpani, bass drum, snare drum, cymbals, and tam-tam—the big gong. There's also a wind machine, used to announce the presence of divine forces, Pan, and the nymphs. A live performance of *Daphnis* requires eight percussionists. But in spite of the presence of so many rarely heard percussion instruments, there isn't a moment in the work where the section sounds out of balance, aggressive, excessive, or as adding anything other than the most delicate emphases and shading. The one possible exception is the wind machine, which may seem over the top to you; apparently some conductors don't use it.[7] Even if it does bother you, keep in mind that as you get to know the piece Ravel's discreet and specific application will start to make sense and fit in.

Debussy used a wordless female chorus in his orchestral work *Sirènes*—"Sirens"—third of his Nocturnes for Orchestra, composed between 1897 and 1899. In *Daphnis* Ravel adapted the strangely beautiful sound into his own idiom with assurance and power: surely the four-part chorus singing its wordless vowels makes the single most distinctive and famous tonal contribution to the work. Consisting of the standard grouping of sopranos, contraltos, tenors, and basses, the strange sound of their singing, sometimes with mouths open, sometimes closed, is used to stunning effect throughout the work. Without the singers, the *Danse religieuse* would lack much of its solemn grandeur; and with the eerie a cappella opening to part 2 the composer assigns the chorus the score's strangest passage. Similarly, the chorus's orgasmic groans in the final *Bacchanale* lends that passage much of its wildness and power. There's no other work in the standard repertory where the human voice is employed so variously for harmonic and rhythmic coloring, as a kind of nonhuman utterance, or as a human but inarticulate voice. Ravel's directions in the score call for the chorus to move from the front to the back of the stage, and even offstage, all utterly impractical. (Imagine forty people tramping around during a performance.) When leading *Daphnis* in concert, conductors try to achieve the differences in dynamics the composer wanted simply by raising or reducing the volume of the group as it sits at the rear of the stage.

Musical passion is common enough, but sexuality depicted in music is a dicier topic, and in Ravel's case the *Boléro* is usually the subject of a discussion about musical eroticism. But the one supposed musical orgasm some listen for in the later work seems fairly pale alongside the *Bacchanale*'s moaning choruses and multiple moments of an almost palpable ecstasy in the *Lever du jour*, which seems to mark *Daphnis* as the most powerfully erotic of Ravel's orchestral scores. (His most frank expression of sexuality is to be found in *Nahandove*, the opening number of the *Chansons madécasses*, however; see pages 142–143.) The shadow of the horned, goat-footed, pipe-playing, half-wild god Pan—"this dangerous presence dwelling just beyond the protected zone of the village boundary"[8]—looms over the work, reflected by the Ravel's awe-struck depictions of the divinity, but also in the sexuality that Pan symbolizes and liberates in the ballet's human characters.

For all the work's gravitational pull, its affects and aesthetics are not easily characterized. In *Daphnis*, Ravel creates sounds that are so beautiful that the listener is seduced by its surfaces; yet in spite of its lovely curves, the work is strange, mysterious, and anything but superficial. The music offers articulate, if playfully detached expression to emotion, such as Daphnis' jealousy in part 1, or Chloé's despair while a prisoner. One moment where deeper feeling is permitted, if only momentarily, is in part 3 when the lovers are reunited. The key moment where nature is given voice—the *Lever du jour*—is obviously of enormous affective impact, and again not just for the beauty of its surfaces. In the score, the composer's heading for the concluding *Bacchanale* is actually *Danse générale*, as all the characters onstage join in a merging that's impersonal, yet also a clear depiction of the erotic. Daphnis and Chloé themselves are merely stick figures, the stock young lovers of a thousand myths and stories. But the urges they represent are potent, and so Ravel's music is not just beautiful but disturbingly powerful. The individuals themselves may mean little, but Nature and Eros, the mighty and indifferent forces that steer them, are depicted, not indifferently, but mightily.

Daphnis et Chloé seems to spring from silence with rumblings on the timpani and low strings. But the dynamics rise as the horns mutter a five-note phrase in a haunting long-shot-long-short-long rhythm that acts as the chief unifying element through the work. A solo flute sings a long, articulate phrase over the over wordless chorus, which repeats the horns' figure in its strange sonority. The oboe, playing high in its range, picks up the flute's long utterance, as the composer thickens the orchestral textures gradually below. Shimmering violins majestically present the characters, who set out on the first choreographic number, the *Danse religieuse*, characterized by rolling triplets for the string section punctuated by decisive chords for the harps, and a tone of solemn ecstasy. Ravel moves his melodic phrases to the woodwinds, as the chorus adds its strange, ineffable spaciousness to the tonal fabric. The crotale punctuates the long phrases, cutting through the rich textures with its distinctive high-pitched clang. Over violin pizzicati, the woodwinds, including the alto flute, trade solos. The triplets take on a more powerfully characterized swaying rhythm, as the full orchestra and chorus play the dance motif in rich *fortissimo*; a violin solo, imitating the earlier ones for the high woodwinds, accompany the entrance of the hero and heroine, who throw themselves down in worship.

Igor Stravinsky, Ravel's friend and colleague, described *Daphnis et Chloé* as "one of the loveliest works of French music."[9] The dance that follows, for young women followed by a "danse générale," is set to a brittle short-short-long theme introduced by the trumpet that is probably the most Stravinskian idea in the work. Ravel's delicate treatment is entirely his own, though. The tapping theme sits with reasonable ease on an uncommon 7/4 beat, but a twisting theme introduced by the woodwinds sounds as though it's limping, as does the beautiful waltzlike passage that follows. Ravel combines all three ideas (tapping, twisting, and pseudo-waltz) quite grandly in a first "danse générale," the richness of which, except for its peculiar rhythm, anticipates *La Valse.* As in many such passages in Ravel, you feel that something's slightly off balance, but without a look at the score you can't quite tell that the beat is source of the disruption.

In the next sequence, the music depicts the attempts of the cowherd Dorcon to sideline Daphnis and kiss Chloé. His grotesque dance is set to a pounding beat for the drums and the gurgling timbre of the three bassoons. A slashing figure for the winds further illustrates Dorcon's clumsiness. In a not unexpected contrast, the dance of Daphnis that follows displays a purer elegance and grace. In this complex bit of ensemble writing, Ravel uses solo brass instruments, notably a rising figure of the horn, to evoke Daphnis's masculine energy; but the trumpets, then more comically a solo trombone, show a spasmodic character that reflects his annoyed mocking of Dorcon. Ravel depicts the laughter of the crowd at Dorcon with bold trills for the horns and sharp-edged figures for the brass and winds. In the long passage that follows, Daphnis rests as the old shepherdess Lyceion stumbles on him and tries to provoke or seduce him in a convulsive musical narration. Like Salome, Lyceion sheds several veils, which Daphnis returns to her with distaste. In the midst of the comedy, phrases of extreme delicacy and great beauty depict her dance.

Lyceion's dance dissolves amid young people fleeing pirates across the stage, to relatively menacing music. Little sense of real danger or direct, powerful emotion penetrates the pure, artful fantasy of these pages. Fearing that the pirates have taken Chloé, Daphnis faints in grief at the feet of statues of three nymphs. Eerie string tremolos accompany "Asiatic" solos for flute, horn, and clarinet as the three nymphs, who act as the deus ex machina—divine intervention—come magically to life, one after another. The wind machine makes its first appearance, and, as noted, you may not like it; but it represents a divine wind, like those heard by ancient Greek and Roman sibyls and prophets. The nymphs then dance, to slow, swaying murmurs that continue the looping figuration for the flutes over continued soft string tremolos; scampering downward figures for the strings amplify the magical mood. Oboes and clarinets continue the figuration, as the music speaks in tones of dizzy wonderment. Clarinets and violas join a fervent phrase leading into a leisurely sequence of rising trills for the strings as the awakened Daphnis prostrates himself before the nymphs; the first part of the ballet ends mysteriously on the steady motion of rising trills for the strings.

The three-minute passage for chorus that opens the second part of *Daphnis* might be the weirdest music Ravel ever wrote. If you feel uneasy or unmoored listening to it, you're not alone; many listeners are reminded of the music of the contemporary Viennese school—Schoenberg, Berg, and Webern, by its daring chromatic shifts. Its delivery at low volume and a slow tempo makes the passage even harder to grasp, but the music should make more sense after a few hearings. The brass fanfares that enter at about two minutes in also help to anchor the ear. These strange tones depict supernatural forces that have been summoned, and, presumably, the unease of Daphnis as he worries about Chloé. Slithering figures for the strings serve to move the narrative along, and a sharp chord for the full orchestra introduces the next section, the pirates' dance. Despite the great racket Ravel conjures, the music is all affect, with no sense of genuine menace: the preceding choral passage can be far more unsettling. But the orchestral writing is striking, with fast, difficult passages for the horns and trumpets. The composer speeds up in the middle section, where, over flying string pizzicati, which soon shifts into a nervous, light bowing, the woodwinds, including the dusky-toned alto flute and the trumpet trade solos with oriental flavoring. Ravel builds a breathless running phrase into an uproarious climax, as the tenors and basses of the chorus enter with a panting figure.

Chloé is brought onstage by her pirate captors and forced to dance; she makes several attempts at escape, all of which are frustrated. The melodic material of her supplicant's dance to the pirate chief is mostly delivered plaintively by the woodwinds, while the music's discontinuous character is set by the plot, Chloé's actions and those of the pirates. But her growing desperation is well depicted in the tightening phrases and thickening orchestral textures Ravel employs. Everything changes abruptly though, as Pan makes his presence felt with spooky and hallucinatory incarnations. At first, as satyrs invade the pirates' camp, Ravel's music may seem conventionally Halloween-ish, with harps sweeping upward against stiffly phrased falling figures for the winds and brass. One passage featuring a clattering xylophone is quite reminiscent of Saint-Saëns's *Danse macabre*. But then Ravel takes a new, more alarming tack as the low-pitched instruments groan out a somber three-note figure. The wind machine tells us that a god is present; and the chorus joins in, scarily. The pirates flee in terror, ending part 2 of the ballet.

Part 3 (CD Tracks 6–8) of *Daphnis et Chloé* opens with its most famous passage, the *Lever du jour*. There are numerous dawns portrayed in music, such as Wagner's in the opera *Götterdämmerung*, and others by Haydn, Rossini, Verdi, and Richard Strauss, but Ravel's spectacular movement stands securely among the greatest and the best known. He may have felt suspicion of Wagner's overwhelming influence in tone painting, but even if this passage owes the German a debt in its breadth and orchestral brilliance, it sounds only like Ravel. Indeed, the composer works on a grand scale, taking an unhurried—for him—seven minutes to let his scheme unfold. The *Lever du jour* stands as one of the greatest examples of tone painting by a master of the art.

Looping scales for the harps and arpeggios traded among the flutes and clarinets, at a slow tempo and low volume open the passage in mystery and magic. Grumblings deep in the cellos and double basses hint at a theme that's forming but unformed; three solo violins imitate with trills and delicate grace notes the chirping of birds that accompany the dawn. A flute, singing a longer, more eloquent chant, joins, as do many winds, in a rich mix of melody and figuration. These lead to a mellow climax on the fragmentary melody that has been assembling itself in the low strings, brass, and winds. It's easy to imagine that you're witnessing a gradually breaking dawn.

Ravel drops the volume as the looping figuration continues, gradually allowing the great melodic span gently to unspool, beginning in the clarinets and violas. Scanning as long-long-short-short-long, but even the "shorts" being long-breathed, the melody, immense yet infinitely supple, opens as though delivered by a higher consciousness, or a voice of nature. Built shrewdly on expanding phrases, the melodic structure is remarkable not only for its beauty and grandeur but for its flexibility: the composer shortens and lengthens it freely as he develops the architecture of the passage, and you'll hear that after each of its several climaxes, the melody seems to start again, as though forming itself anew each time.

Ravel interrupts a flow that seems unstoppable with two woodwind calls, the first for a flute in another birdsonglike phrase; the second, a clarinet depicting a shepherd as he crosses the stage. The second interruption moves to a distant key from which the music now has to find its way sweetly back. By now the melodic line has extended and expanded into an urgent rising phrase; the chorus joins as the violins now sing the melody in its full, extended glory. Shepherds come on the scene, as the anxious lovers are reunited, their tension and worry beforehand expressed in contracted phrases for the violas and clarinets, then violins backed by the cry of the oboe. No musical lovers' meeting can ever sound the same after *Tristan und Isolde*, and that of Daphnis and Chloé possesses a Wagnerian intensity, but also Ravelian concision, passing in a glorious moment.

Ravel hasn't finished yet, however, as a mysterious key change and lowering of dynamics and thinning of the textures allows him to build toward one final climax on the arching melody, marked by delicate percussion eruptions, spinning harps, and impressive commentary from the chorus, which sings the haunting motto theme. He winds the arpeggios down, then shifts the rhythm gently. To a bleating phrase for the oboe set in a traditionally pastoral rhythm, the old shepherd Lammon suggests that to honor the god who reunited them, the lovers should reenact the love story of Pan and the nymph Syrinx in his honor.

This they do in the next scene, where Daphnis and Chloé dance the story. A long, elaborate flute solo of studied melancholy marks this passage, as Daphnis mimes Pan's playing the instrument, while the harps and sharp leaping figures for the piccolo and the strings depict the leaps that are supposed to be happening onstage. The god's pursuit of the fleeing nymph is portrayed in quick, accelerating phrases. Although the flute's solo is long and difficult, the orchestral textures here remain light and the mood is playful throughout this elegant interlude between the intensity of the sunrise and the wild brilliance of the closing section.

The *Bacchanale* opens with a passage in a broad tempo as Daphnis offers two sheep in gratitude to Pan. The work's motto appears majestically, sighed out by the strings, lower brass, and woodwinds above as the trumpets rap out a noble phrase of their own. Daphnis is interrupted by young women, entering to a scampering rhythm, actually the motto theme in a compressed and accelerated guise, ready to begin the rite, which Ravel runs into long, irregular measures. Its primary theme is a breathless skirling figure first given by the winds captures the ecstasy of the dance. This immediately sets the orchestra off into a controlled frenzy that tears on at a fierce pace right to the end. The irregular beat returns, once again making the music seem to stumble forward. Ravel also deploys a full array of his percussion, here more emphatically, as the music demands. There's a crunching climax on two massive chords, but no slackening of the tempo, as the composer holds to the savage pace. The chorus adds wild, inarticulate cries that sound more and more like panting as the dance progresses. Ravel tightens the beat twice, first to 3/4, then to 2/4, as the phrases crush together toward the long-held final breath, uttered by the chorus and the full orchestra.

Ravel's mode for this extraordinary passage may have been Hector Berlioz, a nineteenth-century French composer with an unmistakable and distinctive style. Two of Berlioz's important symphonic works—the *Symphonie fantastique* and *Harold en Italie*—end with wild dances, the first with a much admired witches' Sabbath, while *Harold* concludes with an *Orgie de brigands*—a "Bandits' Orgy." Ravel had mixed feelings about Berlioz's music, which he found deficient from a technical standpoint,[10] but the thematic and rhythmic compression toward the end of Ravel's *Bacchanale* resembles that of the witches' Sabbath, and both end on long-held, high-pitched chords, while the flow and overall character of Ravel's finale is reminiscent of the *Orgie de brigands.*

Daphnis et Chloé, Suites 1 and 2

As mentioned, Ravel extracted two suites of material while working on the ballet. He may have done so due to the unwieldy forces needed for the full ballet, although both suites involve full orchestral and choral complements; or perhaps he believed that the extracts would find more frequent performance, which in fact they have. The Suite No. 2, as noted, is more popular than No. 1, by a ratio of almost ten to one, if the ArkivMusic.com website that offers ninety-nine performances of No. 2 to eleven of No. 1 gives an accurate indication. None of part 1 of the ballet is included in the suites, which takes the second part as the first suite, and part 3 as the second. The first suite begins with "Nymph's Dances," which are called *Nocturne.* This is followed by the a cappella choral passage that opens part 2 of the ballet, here referred to as *Interlude.* It's concluded by the pirates' dance, here called the *Danse guerrière*—"Warrior's Dance." Ravel assembled this sequence before finishing the ballet, but that strange choral interlude is the least likely part of the score to win friends. Suite No. 2, on the other hand (CD Tracks 6–8), opens with the *Lever du jour*; continues with the Pan and Syrinx dance, here called the *Pantomime*; and ends with the thrilling *Danse générale*, the so-called *Bacchanale.* This suite, which moves from strength to strength, was clearly headed for popular success.

La Valse

Ravel wrote the work with the intention that the Ballets Russes would produce and perform it, but, as mentioned earlier, the company's manager Diaghilev demurred, offending Ravel irreparably. Standing in opposition to the *Boléro*, *La Valse* is admired universally for its aesthetics and execution. This sardonic tone poem of 1920 seems the later work's inversion: although the former seems hardly to budge, *La Valse* flies ahead breathlessly; the *Boléro* is a strange if fascinating study, and *La Valse* is a working text in the deployment of the symphony orchestra. As he would with *Boléro*, Ravel provided a text to explain the piece, although in both cases the music extends far beyond his verbal parameters:

> Through clouds whirling around, flashes of light permit us to see waltzing couples. They thin out; by and by we can see an immense hall crowded with a rotating throng. The stage gets progressively brighter. Lights from chandeliers burst from the ceiling. An imperial court, about 1855.[11]

Anyone who has heard *La Valse* knows that the work is spectral and shadowy, building toward a catastrophic ending, which the composer doesn't mention in his sketch. Whereas instrumental music is generally best approached on its own merits, tone poems like the *Symphonie fantastique* by Berlioz or those by Richard Strauss tell stories in music. Unlike Strauss's and Berlioz's works, *La Valse* lacks specific incident, but its progress and message have a narrative character.

Ravel's work is another extraordinary summary of waltz suites from Schubert, Schumann, Chopin, Johann Strauss, Richard Strauss, and, of course, by Ravel himself, in the *Valses nobles et sentimentales*, which sound almost innocent alongside the savagery of this. Typical waltzes of the nineteenth century are compilations of several dances, as in Schubert's sets; Schumann's *Papillons*; Chopin's *Grande Valse brillante*, published as Op. 18, a big multipart waltz; and Johann Strauss's, clearly suites, none single dances. Richard Strauss wrote a famously anachronistic waltz into his operatic comedy set in eighteenth-century Vienna, *Der Rosenkavalier*. And many Mahler symphonies (the First, Second,

Seventh, and Ninth) contain waltzlike movements that may be innocent, sardonic, or both. Others (the Third, Fourth, Fifth, and Sixth) have dance movements that aren't precisely waltzes, but come close.[12] In every case, Mahler uses them as a way to look back at a time that seemed more innocent. Even though the form may be well populated, Ravel's cataclysmic work stands as perhaps its most radical example.

Yet although fairly complex from a formal standpoint, *La Valse* is in no sense difficult to grasp: you'll understand it on first listening without having to read this or any analysis, including Ravel's. What make it remarkable are the composer's stunning orchestral mastery and his skill at presenting fragments, putting them together, then taking them apart in a sequence that operates according to its own musical and dramatic rules. The piece opens with a mysterious introduction, which recurs twice later; otherwise it's a waltz suite that Ravel brings to two climaxes, the second and final one disastrous. His setting makes clear that terrible forces have swept away the "imperial courts of 1855" along with their dancers. We can safely extrapolate from its post–World War I date that the composer correctly viewed that world as gone forever, expressing his view in this model of concision—it's only eleven or twelve minutes long. With the sweep and grandeur of its pacing, *La Valse* carries the listener along relentlessly, speaking plainly to the doom-laden side in all of us.

Ravel's tempo marking, "*Mouvement de Valse viennoise*"—"In the tempo of a Viennese waltz"—speaks with the same bare and savage irony as the title, seemingly generic, without a hint of the work's dark tone. But the inchoate growls from the double basses that open the piece are anything but comforting. The familiar three-beat pulse tries to coalesce, as the bassoons, horns, and clarinets suggest a waltz heard from a distance, but again, strange, fluttering runs for the flutes and clarinets also raise alarm. After some sweeps by the two harps, which the composer keeps quite busy throughout *La Valse*, a full waltz tune now emerges in the violins, but softly and in midphrase, making us feel we're approaching a ballroom.

After about two and one-half minutes of such preparation, a complete, swooping waltz tune finally emerges at full volume. This is succeeded by a contrasting dance, a loopy, more lyrical melody first stated by the oboe, then the strings. Here the tone, while no longer as strange or menacing as the opening, remains cool, and the roar of the full orchestra anticipates greater rages to come. The whirring scales played by the woodwinds in the introduction now come back as integral parts of the instrumental textures. The oboe plays its loopy tune again, and, just like in a waltz suite by Johann Strauss, a contrasting dance in a sharper rhythm follows. Heavy percussion punctuates the climaxes of the phrases, and chromatic shifts in the harmony, and weird trills for the horns begin to suggest disruption.

The opening phrase comes back, now comprehensible in its full statement, but still oddly disturbing. A schmaltzy dance in a classic waltz-type phrase (short-short-long) led by two solo violins echoed by the flutes changes the tone, but sounding unmistakably saccharine and false. A long, scampering dance for the flutes should please but doesn't because their rhythm and harmony are off, and again, the trilling horns unnerve. Ravel brings back the opening dance, now alarming once more as it's growled out by the bassoons, and the flutes play their running scales, which also sound off-kilter: the music is unquestionably losing its bearings, and taking ours, with it. The transition from strange to normal, then back to strange, is accompanied with uncanny subtlety and speed. By now everything seems odd: the trumpet takes the loopy tune, and climaxes are thunderous, but harmonies tell us that something's wrong. Phrases succeed each other out of order, broken up and stood on their heads, leaping down instead of up. The opening phrase comes back once more, but a rising chromatic line tracks our alarm as the waltz phrases return, hideously distorted, blowing apart. The dances try to reassert themselves, but a greater force has taken over and tosses them around. The final pages represent the scrambling attempts of the waltz to come back, and to find itself, but massive eruptions from the brass smash the dance to bits.

Boléro

Ravel composed his most famous work, the *Boléro*, in 1928. Some listeners who think of themselves as serious consider it no more than a stunt, and as musical trash. So, here it may be worth quoting his own explanation in a letter to a friend:

> It is an experiment in a very special and limited direction, and should not be suspected of aiming at achieving anything different from, or anything more than, it actually does achieve. Before the first performance, I issued a warning to the effect that what I had written was a piece lasting seventeen minutes and consisting wholly of orchestral tissue without music—of one long, very gradual crescendo. There are no contrasts, and there is practically no invention except in the plan and the manner of the execution. The themes are impersonal—folk tunes of the usual Spanish-Arabian kind. Whatever may be said to the contrary, the orchestral treatment is simple and straightforward throughout, without the slightest attempt at virtuosity.[13]

So, assuming Ravel's comment to be straightforward, the work was to him a singular experiment. We may take issue with his description of the piece as being "without the slightest attempt at virtuosity" since it's unquestionably a rare feat, but to call it a stunt seems to go too far. He composed nothing that doesn't contain at least a hint of irony, but the *Boléro* seems far too elaborate and carefully assembled to be called an out-and-out joke. Although the *Boléro* is not a piece one can hear every day, the best way to approach it is to listen with an open mind and decide for yourself on its merits.

Its structure is laughably simple, not even adequate to be called a theme and variations. Two long, sinuous, closely related melodies are stated softly at the outset at a moderate tempo that never changes; nor does the three-beat meter. They are alternated in eighteen strictly ordered, paired iterations, absolutely unvaried except for a thickening of the instrumental texture, and two key changes of earth-shaking effect just before the end. It's also famously subjected to what must be the longest, most carefully calculated crescendo—steady increase in volume—in music. But, of course, there's more to it than that, and we'll see how Ravel plays with our expectations of music—and our nervous systems—to make the *Boléro* work.

The *Boléro* opens with a delicate tapping on the snare drum of a rhythm that one can hear as irresistible or maddening; this exact pattern continues all the way to the end. Cellos and violas add the simpler beats elaborated by the snare. The flute then plays the first tune, plain, but with interesting stamping figures worked in. It's in two long phrases, with a call and response quality reminiscent of flamenco performance. Although it's not the most memorable or characterful melody ever written, it doesn't have to be, for obvious reasons. The clarinet gently plays its second iteration. The second tune, played by the bassoon, has more personality, with triplets that intensify the rhythm and an insistent repeated note that tugs persistently at the melody and harmony. This second melody, with its altered rhythm and slight pull from the nominal harmonic structure, plays a crucial role in broadening the piece, and making it less monotonous. A clarinet repeats this tune. The nasal oboe d'amore, called *hautbois d'amour* in the score, plays the opening tune, replied to by the flute doubled by a muted trumpet. All the while, Ravel thickens the rhythmic accompaniment very gradually, having, for example, the harp join the strings and the flute double the snare drum in tapping out the rhythm. He has also raised the volume incrementally and gently from *pianissimo*—very soft—to *piano*—soft—to a rarely used *mezzo piano*—medium soft—that shows the range of expressive resources the composer needs to pull his feat off. The alternating sequences continue, with Ravel introducing relatively unusual instruments to the orchestra as well as strange combinations. Among the former are saxophones, the oily tone of which sits oddly on top of the textures of the orchestra. A trombone takes the second, insistent tune with sleazy slips and slides. The most bizarre instrumental and harmonic combination comes in the eighth iteration, as two piccolos, each playing in a different key, a horn playing in its strangled highest register, and the celesta join in an unforgettably weird moment. By this point, Ravel has added a horn to the snare and flute as they tap out the rhythm, and they dynamics are up to a steady *piano*.

By the ninth iteration, the high winds join to blare the opening theme out over a more elaborate accompaniment for the strings softly playing sweeping triplets; by the twelfth, the violins join the high winds in the first tune as the volume has now been advanced to *forte*—loud. By this point, the plain rhythm originally taken by the violas and cellos is barked out by ever-swelling instrumental groups, including bassoons, horns, and timpani, and the melodies are shrieked out. By the sixteenth iteration, the tunes are played in coarse harmony, and everyone (not including the celesta, however) not playing the melodic material is banging out one part or another of the rhythmic accompaniment. Ravel holds his *coup de théâtre* for the last moment, as he takes the key from the C major, where the entire piece has been, into a few cataclysmic moments into E major, and over some famous yawps for the trombones and saxophones he wrenches back to the home key, another shattering effect, as the whole orchestra seems to lurch into the closing cadence in the first and only change of rhythm in the entire work. So, Ravel saves all of his big effects for the *Boléro*'s final minute.

The question always asked about the *Boléro* concerns its supposedly sexual nature: is it really an attempt at a musical depiction of coitus? Ravel himself described the work's "musico-sexual element,"[14] and of course its long buildup to a big climax is clear. Watching the final moments of the dance in the 1934 film of the same title, one might be persuaded that music is such a portrayal. But there it's really the choreography and the performances of Carole Lombard and George Raft that make that impression. The quickening ebb and flow of sex are not to be found: it may be better to think of the *Boléro* as a slow burn rendered into music. What also solidified the perception—by now long a cliché—of the *Boléro* as a background track for sex was its use in the 1979 film comedy *10*, directed by Blake Edwards. (Watching *10* is an object lesson in how badly a once-popular movie can age.) As we know from *Nahandove*, the first of the *Chansons madécasses*, Ravel was quite capable of depicting sexual excitement in music.

It's also worth noting that Ravel supposedly said that the *Boléro* was "my masterpiece . . . too bad there isn't any music in it,"[15] a comment so conveniently ironic that one has to question whether he really said it.

Perhaps the most sensible way to think of the *Boléro* is to consider Ravel's overall style, thinking also of the *Tzigane*, another polished Ravelian take on a rough model, that of the Hungarian rhapsody type. *Boléro* is surely cut from a similar, Spanish pattern. Leaving aside as disingenuous his remark that it contains "not the slightest attempt at virtuosity," we can look at it as yet another sophisticated work by a supremely refined musical imagination. It's also a test and display piece for an orchestra, especially the percussionist who carries the work from start to finish. Surely it's a feat, and not merely a stunt.

Curiously, few recordings of the *Boléro* are as slow as the composer wanted it; even that conducted by Pierre Monteux, who worked with Ravel, runs 15:20, rather than the "seventeen minutes" Ravel mentions in his note, quoted earlier. YouTube carries two performances that move at the stately tempo Ravel wanted: a recent one with the Vienna Philharmonic under Gustavo Dudamel and one made in 1930 of the Lamoureux Orchestra, conducted by Piero Coppola, made in the composer's presence and under his supervision.

8 The Operas

Although works of unquestionable merit and even of greatness, Ravel's two operas are peculiar, standing well apart from mainstream operatic tradition. Both works, *L'Heure espagnole*—"The Spanish Hour"—and *L'Enfant et les sortilèges*—"The Child and the Spells"—toy with and subvert audience expectations. Although as complex as any of the greatest operatic works, both have performance times that run under an hour. There's no vocal display to speak of in *L'Heure espagnole*; *L'Enfant et les sortilèges* has some, but nothing like what we might hear in a mainstream late romantic era work by Massenet, Puccini, or Richard Strauss. Certainly Ravel's operas will puzzle and disappoint those looking for broad, *Pagliacci*-esque tunes and melodrama. Like everything he wrote, these works are intensely focused on their themes, which are narrow—an hour in the love life of an eighteenth-century Spanish woman—to somewhat broader, the consciousness and impulses of a child. But, of course, both are of high refinement; in both Ravel skillfully welds short scenes into larger structures. The twenty-one nominal scenes that make up *L'Heure espagnole* are fused in a straightforward progress toward a climactic (offstage) sexual encounter between two of its five characters, then a concluding ensemble for all. The action of *L'Enfant et les sortilèges* is broken by various divertissement-like interludes that digress artfully from the opera's movement toward its touching final moments.

French writers and poets of the turn of the twentieth century liked poetic, allusive titles that often translate awkwardly into English. The busy action of the Spanish sex comedy takes place over the hour that the main character's husband is out setting the municipal clocks of Toledo. Then why isn't it *Une Heure espagnole*, "A Spanish Hour"? The vocal score of *L'Enfant et les sortilèges* translates the title as "The Bewitched Child," which, although helpfully concise, isn't quite correct: that would be *L'Enfant ensorcelé*. As with Proust's novelistic epic *À la Recherche du temps perdu*—"In Search of Lost Time"—translators must decide whether to use a literal rendering, or, as with R. Scott Moncrieff's first translation into English, "Remembrance of Things Past," to find less accurate but more poetic titles that evoke the spirit of the original.

In any case, it's best when approaching Ravel's two operas, odd but brilliant, to stay humble and keep an open mind. Certainly *L'Enfant et les sortilèges*, with its broader subject, has wider appeal, and probably represents the greater achievement of the two. But don't think for a moment that *L'Heure espagnole* is a dud, or not worth getting to know. Indeed, the opposite is true. Compositions of great refinement, both demand much of listeners and viewers who admire Ravel's stylistic mastery, and both will repay your attention and acquaintance over time.

L'Heure espagnole

Ravel composed this sly comedy between 1907 and 1909 to a libretto by Maurice Étienne Legrand, who worked under the pen name Franc-Nohain. It was first performed in Paris in 1911. Five characters inhabit the work, which has a simple plot:

Concepcion, the wife of the eighteenth-century Toledo watchmaker Torquemada, has taken as potential lovers two disappointments: Gonzalve, a poetic bachelor, and Don Inigo Gomez, a pompous old banker, both of whom visit the watchmaker's shop during the hour Torquemada is out setting the municipal clocks. Gonzalve can only spout romantic rubbish, while Don Inigo sings conventional phrases of seduction, but soon tires out. But as the at-first-unwelcome mule driver Ramiro helps Concepcion move clocks (and even the two would-be lovers hidden inside clocks), an attraction grows between the two. Concepcion finally invites Ramiro to her bedroom "*sans horloge*"—without a clock. Torquemada returns, sells the two embarrassed pretenders the expensive timepieces in which they hid, and all five characters join to sing a brief, brilliant closing ensemble.

The opera's twenty-one tiny scenes occupy a playing time of barely more than forty-five minutes; and performances (live and recorded) of this remarkable work are few. The scene divisions mean little, as the music and action are tight and fluent. Yet apart from the work's eccentricity from an operatic standpoint, getting to know *L'Heure espagnole* can be really rewarding. You might read that in the opera Ravel treats humans like machines, and that the work has a detached posture, but such analyses should be taken with a grain of salt; listen, or better, watch (it's available on DVD and on YouTube) and make up your own mind. Although nominally about sex, there's certainly little of the conventionally erotic in this brittle, intentionally superficial opera.

Ravel's pupil, conductor Manuel Rosenthal, describes the score as "*by far* the most sophisticated of all his work,"[1] quite a statement when you think of the former's achievements as an orchestrator. Rosenthal also correctly points out that the size of the orchestra, as well as the need for numerous rehearsals, make the opera expensive and impractical to produce, another obstacle to more frequent performances. Indeed, the almost Straussian (as in Richard) richness and sophistication of the orchestral part of *L'Heure espagnole* become more apparent—and more astonishing—with each hearing. Ravel's orchestra is very large, requiring, as he often does, a percussion section of exceptional size and range, and the score demands high-level playing, so the work's orchestral glories lie beyond the scope of amateur companies, though they can, of course, use the piano reduction.

The opening passage, set to the ticking of three clocks, displays many of the opera's virtues, as low winds and brass join muted cellos, the bells, celesta, and other percussion, all deployed with rare delicacy, to paint an aurally rich portrait of the watchmaker's shop; it's worth noting, too, that Ravel changes the beat in almost every bar for the first minute or so, and then less regularly but still freely. Until the final quintet, in which the characters join to sing the moral, the work consists of alternating dialogues for two and sometimes three characters, alternating with declaimed monologues so brief that they cannot be considered arias. Ravel's musical characterizations are witty: although he's introduced by a stately rhythm recalling the French overture of the baroque era, Don Inigo makes his feeble attempt at seduction to a waltz, like Baron Ochs in Strauss's *Der Rosenkavalier* (Ravel preceded the more famous work by Strauss by two years, though it was staged later). Once he has given up, he confesses, to the unusual accompaniment of the tuba, that he'd much rather be "*chez soi, dans un large fauteuil, les pieds dans ses pantoufles*"—"at home, in an easy chair, my feet in their slippers." The bachelor poet Gonzalve sings in ludicrously ornamented lines, or, as in his second monologue ("*En dépit de cette inhumaine*"—"In spite of this cruel woman"), with the winds and strings underlining his hyperbole with wild, looping figuration.

Concepcion, the character around whom the action spins, sings in a mixture of patter and straightforward declaimed line, with few lyrical outbursts or high notes. Her expression of frustration, "*Oh, la pitoyable aventure!*"—"What a pathetic adventure"—ends with a brilliant, flamenco flavored commentary in the form of a cadenza for the bassoon, which, like the tuba, rarely gets a solo. The mule driver Ramiro receives the most openly sympathetic treatment; his first short monologue accompanied by tender strings and winds, and for the second, "*Voilà ce que j'appelle une femme charmante*"—"Now that's what I call a charming woman"—in which he envies the watchmaker his life, work, and wife, Ravel brings back the music of the magical introductory passage. The composer's mastery of Spanish musical idiom means that the score is generously flavored with Spanish rhythm and melody, but these are deployed strictly for color, not to make *L'Heure espagnole* into a would-be Spanish opera: rather, it's unmistakably an opera by Ravel.

Spanish coloring reaches its height in the final quintet, "*Un financier . . . et un poète . . . un époux ridicule . . .*"—"A financier . . . and a poet . . . a ridiculous husband"—set in the characteristic and irresistible swaying rhythm of a habanera, which is not only the high point of the score, but a tribute to Spanish music (in it Ravel quotes his own *Alborada del gracioso*). In this remarkable conclusion, all of three minutes long, the five singers move to the front of the stage, no longer in character but not fully out, either, to sing the moral, that in the pursuit of love "*Le muletier a son tour*"—"The muleteer has his turn." Here the twining, showy vocal lines demand careful coordination. The ensembles that end Mozart's *Don Giovanni* and *Così fan tutte* clearly served as Ravel's models here, as both musical dramatists signal the end of the proceedings with relatively lighthearted summings-up by the cast, which now steps away from its puppetlike roles. This type of conclusion (which also can be found in Verdi's *Falstaff*) lets us know that the work has been governed by artifice rather than realism.

L'Enfant et les sortilèges

Although it observes more operatic conventions than *L'Heure espagnole*, "The Child and the Spells" remains well on the eccentric side. Composed between 1920 and 1925, the work premiered in Monte Carlo in the latter year. The choreographer was twenty-year-old George Balanchine, in his first important commission. And this time, Ravel's collaborator was Colette (born Sidonie-Gabrielle Colette), one of the most revered French writers of the twentieth century. Despite moments of preciousness, Colette's rhapsodic text is set at an altogether higher pitch than that of *L'Heure espagnole*. Although this second opera has by necessity a playful side, Ravel and Colette address with rare insight the child protagonist's consciousness as he lurches from willfulness, grandiosity, and cruelty to terror of the natural and adult worlds and consequent recognition of his small size and weakness. The fifty-minute work ekes out an ending that's only ambiguously happy.

Again, the plot is simple: A bored boy of six or seven defies his mother's instructions to work on his lessons; as punishment he is instructed to stay in his room, where most of the opera is set. Enraged, he shrieks his contempt of her and everyone, defiantly declaring himself *méchant*—"naughty." He knocks over dishes and furniture, and attacks his pets, a caged squirrel and a cat. But the occupants of his room, first inanimate, afterward sentient, accuse, indict, and cut him down to size. At first the boy is merely terrified, then exhausted by his trials. But all forgive him when he quietly shows pity for a wounded animal. He is returned to his mother, and in the closing line of the opera the boy calls to her. Besides the child, the only other human to appear in the work is the mother, who isn't seen but portrayed as a giant shadow, and sung just offstage. The amateur psychoanalyst in all who know about Ravel's close bond with his own mother cannot help but believe that behind this *ur*-mother, tender but also terrifying, is the shadow of Marie Delouart Ravel.

Titled a "*fantaisie lyrique*"—"lyric fantasy"—Ravel's score is a landmark of twentieth-century music. Despite the composer's description of the work as lyrical, his music shows a firm grasp of progressive musical directions of the 1920s, with much dissonance and a hard, dry, bright sound we might associate with Stravinsky's contemporaneous music. Although here, as throughout his oeuvre, Ravel maintains the purity of his melodic lines, you may be struck by the brittle dissonances in which they are often draped, except at key moments, including the paired arias of the child and the fairy princess and the closing chorus, which receive more mellow harmonic treatment. As in his first opera, the composer deploys a big percussion section, as well as pianos and offstage effects. Here the cast is large, with more than twenty singers required, with vocal demands that are greater than in *L'Heure espagnole*. Even though singers can and are even expected to double up on roles, this complex music drama really benefits from the resources of a large or medium-size company.

L'Enfant begins with a tranquil but rhythmically irregular orchestral introduction for two oboes and a single double-bass, followed by a brief monologue for the child, played by a soprano: "*J'ai pas envie de faire ma page*"—"I don't want to learn my lesson"—the scene between the child and his mother that sets the plot in motion. The mother sings with tenderness, then with just a bit more severity after the boy shows his defiance, although she does try to make him feel guilty: "*Songez surtout au chagrin de*

Maman"—"Above all think of how sad you've made your mother." His tantrum, set vividly to a violent sequence for piano and woodwinds, sets up the scenes that follow, which are mostly brief, broken here and there by choreographic and choral interludes.

First, two chairs come to life, singing in formal phrases of the relief they feel now that their tormentor "*aux talons méchants*"—"with wicked heels"—is in disfavor and perhaps on the way out. Then, to the child's astonishment and terror, they perform an archaic, heavy-footed dance. In a driving passage the clock comes alive, singing that all it can do is chime the hours continually; broken by the child, it no longer knows the time. In the next little scene, a black Wedgwood teapot and a Chinese cup broken by the child indulge in a jazz-inflected duet in dialogue that veers from real English words that almost make sense ("*Black and chic, jolly fellow . . .*") to mock-Asian nonsense ("*Mah jong . . . Sessue Hayakawa*," the latter being the name of a once-famous Japanese film actor) to dirty double-entendres embedded in the patter.[2] When watching this scene you have to keep in mind that in the 1920s such ethnic humor was acceptable, and that exotic influences, whether Spanish, American jazz, or "oriental," were common in European music. That said, Ravel renders the sequence impeccably, even amusingly; listen for the mock-schmaltzy trombone solo.

To the accompaniment of trilling strings and pictorial runs for the piano, the fire flares out of the chimney, calls the child "*Petit barbare imprudent*"—"Little savage, bold and reckless"—for overturning the kettle and scattering the matches; the long scale passages for high soprano that depict the flames sound harder than they are in the context of Ravel's relatively undemanding vocal writing. Then, as gray cinders rise behind the fire, fire and smoke play choreographically to more piano arpeggios. Now the terrified child whispers, "*J'ai peur . . .*"—"I'm afraid." Ravel and Colette settle things down with a calmer interlude as the shepherds, shepherdesses, and animals on the wallpaper he has torn join in a pastoral mourning the end of their idyllic existence and of the child's reign of terror, too. They come to life, then perform a leisurely dance in mock-pastoral mode. Set to the accompaniment of light percussion, piano, and woodwinds, the music remains cool, even though it's supposed to show their grief at being dispersed.

The sequential arias for the fairy princess and the child form the central, crucial panel of *L'Enfant*. Sweeping figuration for the harp evokes magic and awe as the child watches the entrance of the golden-haired fairy princess from his favorite storybook. She sings to the accompaniment of a single flute, in a gently swaying rhythm of her importance to him, "*ta première bien-aimée*"—"your first and best love." To a quicker accompaniment of winds, she expresses her fear of being out in the world, away from the safety of the book. The child shares her anxiety, saying that the prince in the story or he himself might help her. But she sings, to the child, "*petit ami trop faible*"—"my weak little friend"—that she is only a dream, then vanishes. Alone and desolate, the child sings of his despair in a tender aria with a spare, chamberlike accompaniment ("*Toi, le coeur de la rose*"—"You, the heart of the rose").

Anyone who has suffered from math anxiety will relate to the next sequence in which numbers, measurements, and problems, led by an old man in a suit covered with numbers and pi on his hat, pursue the child within a witty blend of comedy and terror. Dizzy from the assault, the child complains of his head. The cat whose tail he pulled at the start of the opera appears, but now the child, though frightened, is getting used to the pattern: "*C'est toi, Chat? . . . Tu parles aussi, sans doute?*"—"Is that you, Cat? . . . No doubt you can speak, too?" The cat, joined by a female of his species, engage in a meowing duet of rare mimetic accuracy, leading to an overheated, comical climax. Now the real magic begins, as the walls of the room disappear and the child finds himself in the garden of his home, once familiar but now transformed into a place of wonder and fear.

Ravel now evokes with brilliance the sounds of the garden at night in the score's most magical passage, night music that sounds much like what Bartók wrote. Contemporary with the Hungarian master's early efforts in this kind of tone painting, it's hard to say who influenced whom; either way, Ravel's depiction is an extraordinary though lesser-known example. To a slower tempo, chilly chords for the muted strings set the mood, as woodwinds, including a flute offstage, moan and chirp like insects. The chorus, broken into small groups, now imitates the rhythmical calls of frogs with stunning accuracy and beauty. The child is happy to see the familiar garden, but immediately the trees groan of the wounds he has bestowed on them thoughtlessly with "*le couteau dérobé*"—"that knife you stole." At last moved to pity, the child leans sympathetically against the tree. Dragonflies and moths then begin another choreographic interlude, a slow and melancholy waltz called by Ravel *Valse américaine*. Set mostly for the piano in dissonant arpeggios accompanied by quiet strings, the dance melts into birdcalls, sung by a soprano, and a return of the frogs' wonderful chorus. The dragonfly and bats recall to him members of their species he thoughtlessly pinned and swatted, reminding him that other creatures have families, too.

Another dance, this one for frogs, follows. Set for one horn and the low strings, a cool waltz gives us a moment's pause before the final scene. The child's sneezy pet squirrel, the movements and manners of which Ravel captures with a sharp ear and wit, discusses the boy's misdeeds. The frog, singing in irregular rhythm, knows only of "*la mouche qu'on me jette*"—"the fly he threw to me." The squirrel answers angrily, calling the frog "*sans-cervelle*"—"brainless"—and the child explains to the squirrel that he was caged only so he might be admired. But the squirrel will have none of it. To a final slow waltz the child realizes "*Ils s'aiment . . . Ils sont heureux . . . Ils m'oublient*"—"They love each other . . . they're full of joy . . . they forget me." But all those he has offended now join forces in a brief but noisy assault. Finally they forget the child is there, as a baby squirrel who's been hurt in the uproar falls in front of him; using a ribbon from around his neck, the child now shows active pity, binding the little squirrel's paw.

Singing in strange, hollow voices to a curious march led by the bassoons, the animals realize that he is not the wicked child they thought, but a fellow creature, with a small injury of his own, capable of and therefore deserving pity. They lift him up, try to carry him to the house, and as he calls for his mother, they join his call, even though they don't understand "*le mot qu'il a crié tout à l'heure*"—"the word he was just crying." In a heart-easing hymn ("*Il est bon, l'Enfant, il est sage*"—"The child is good; he is wise") that also displays Ravel's many-faceted technical sophistication, they guide him; the child holds out his arms, and, reconciled to his mother and to his widening world, he sings in a soft, falling cadence, "*Maman.*"

The Works for Voice

The rarefied world of the art song has a small audience that makes up in passion for what it lacks in numbers. Although these songs are not terribly different than the ones by the Gershwins, Smokey Robinson, or Nas that everyone knows, the lyrics that are set to music that's "classical," and are sung to accompaniments that can be as simple or as elaborate as the composer wants. The texts, too, can be plain, as with Ravel's folk song settings, to dense, as with his songs based on poems by Stéphane Mallarmé. Bigger-boned and more vivid than Debussy's fine-grained art songs, Ravel's are easier to appreciate and enjoy. To add to their appeal, quite a few are backed by chamber ensembles or orchestras. As is common for the art song, many are arranged into suites that follow a theme. Ravel composed songs, typically titled *mélodies*, from the start of his career to the very end, with the trio of songs *Don Quichotte à Dulcinée* of 1933 his prematurely final work.

In the groupings of two or more songs that follow a theme you'll find his most significant contributions to the literature. Known as song cycles, these can follow a story line, as in Schubert's *Die schöne Müllerin*—"The Miller's Beautiful Daughter"—where a young apprentice's obsession is followed in twenty short, piercing songs, set to lyrics by Wilhelm Müller. The folklike naïveté of the text and the repetitive patterns of Schubert's music create effects crucial to the cycle's power, while masking the sophistication of both elements. Ravel's forays into folk themes are also highly successful, as he skillfully applies his polished style to straightforward lyrics. Explorations of broader themes, such as the meditations on beauty and its transience in Mahler's *Das Lied von der Erde*—"The Song of the Earth"—form another type of song cycle. Ravel's song cycles, from *Shéhérazade* to his Spanish set based on Cervantes, are similar to Mahler's in that they pursue impressions rather than narrate a story, like Schubert's. As you'll see, exotic and orientalist influences and effects are considerable in this category of Ravel's oeuvre.

If you're listening online, you'll notice that accompaniments may differ, with one song backed by a piano in one performance and an orchestra in another. The reason is that in several cases, Ravel or another musician transcribed the accompaniments, originally for the piano, for orchestra. The famous recording of the Greek folk songs by soprano Victoria de los Angeles features well-made orchestrations by Ravel and his student Manuel Rosenthal. Two song cycles, the *Chansons madécasses* and the settings of the three Mallarmé poems, feature chamber ensembles of meticulously selected instruments as accompaniments, which are the only ones performed. And you'll only hear *Shéhérazade* performed in its glorious orchestral setting.

Big and glamorous, *Shéhérazade* of 1903 is well known, but it's preceded as Ravel's earliest cycle by the less familiar *Épigrammes de Clément Marot*—"Epigrams by Clément Marot"—a poet of the early sixteenth century. Marot's concise, witty lyrics suit the young Ravel well; the composer's style in these two short songs is already in full bloom. In the first, *D'Anne qui me jecta de la neige*—"On Anne, Who Threw Snow at Me"—he deploys archaic harmonies to evoke both the antiquity of the text and the timelessness of its passionate message. The second, *D'Anne jouant de l'espinette*—"On Anne Playing the Spinet"—has a charmingly busy piano part, depicting the girl playing.

A landmark of Ravel's early maturity, *Shéhérazade* needs to be understood as an artifact of high orientalism. Although on their own the perfumed generalizations of the texts by Arthur Leclère under the Wagnerian pen name Tristan Klingsor sound ludicrous, they are sincere and skillfully assembled, and Ravel's treatments bring them to life. Even here, in one of his deepest dips into orientalism, the composer's innate reserve keeps the mock-Asian seasoning within bounds. *Shéhérazade* may not be politically correct, but once you allow Ravel room to work his magic, you'll hear it as another masterwork.

Asie—"Asia" (CD Track 9)—the first and by far longest of the three songs, is set in a quasi-spoken vocal line needed to dispatch Leclère's long, image-heavy poem, reaching climaxes at the high points of the text as Ravel unerringly perceived them. In the poem, the narrator fantasizes a travelogue through quasi-mythical Asian lands. A snaky figure for the oboe that recurs throughout suggests an "oriental" setting as the singer (usually a soprano) expresses desire to visit; quiet, syncopated figures for the winds and strings suggest the movement of water, as a figure in a sharper rhythm for the clarinets the gentle slap of the waves against "*la goëlette*"—"the schooner"—on which the imaginary journey starts out. She then beings the litany of desire, each beginning with the words "*Je voudrais voir*"—"I want to see"—on which Ravel structures the song and builds tension with its repetition. First she imagines Damascus, with its minarets, and "*beaux turbans de soie sur des visages noirs aux dents claires*"—"beautiful silk turbans above black faces with gleaming teeth"—as the orchestra trembles quietly in an excitement that presages ecstasy. The slapping figure returns with more force as the narrator continues longingly through the bazaars, the music reaching its first climax as she sings of "*des cadis, et des vizirs, qui du seul mouvement de leur doigt qui se penche accordent vie ou mort au gré de leur désir*"—"cadis and viziers who by bending their finger, grant life or death, according to their whim"—the orchestra echoing the narrator's excitement with a sharp, stalking rhythm.

The mental traveler moves on to China, as winds and the celesta paint the ancient kingdom where she will find "*les lettrés qui se querellent sur la poésie et sur la beauté*"—"scholars arguing about poetry and beauty"—among other charming sights. But the fantasy, followed by the tone of the accompaniment, quickens and turn dark as she sings of "*assassins souriant*"—"smiling assassins"—as the poem rushes in its broadest language to its greatest climax: "*Je voudrais voir des pauvres et des reines; je voudrais voir des roses et du sang; je voudrais voir mourir d'amour ou bien de haine*"—"I want to see paupers and queens; I want to see roses and blood; I want to see people dying of love, or of hate." Here the music surges on wavelike arpeggios for the strings, the slapping figure, and longer notes for the singer, climaxing on a high B-flat. The words may appear silly, but the grandeur of this moment, expressed with such eloquent music and placed in the setting of this difficult text, are irresistible and rendered moving by Ravel's treatment. The final words form a quiet postlude, returning to the rhythms and cooler instrumental colors that earlier depicted the sea and the ship. Not least among the composer's achievements here is his masterful pacing, which feels unhurried even as he juggles several hundred words through an introduction, what feels like a long buildup, a big climax, then a closing passage, all in about nine minutes.

Asie's two companions are shorter and less dramatic but just as polished. The first, *La Flûte enchantée*—"The Magic Flute"—depicts a servant of uncertain gender listening for the sound of his or her beloved playing the instrument outside while his or her master dozes. Naturally enough, a mysterious flute solo dominates the orchestra, rising to a climax on the phrase "*Et j'écoute au dehors une chanson de flûte où s'épanche tour à tour la tristesse ou la joie*"—"And I listen to the song of the flute, expressing sadness and joy in turn." Ravel devises another impressive, unrhetorical closing, again placing the flute in the foreground. In the third song, *L'Indifférent*—"The Unresponsive One"—a narrator apostrophizes an adolescent boy he or she is admiring in the street. The music moves at a slow, even pace, as the singer describes the boy's androgynous beauty, then, to a longing phrase for the clarinet, observes, "*Ta lèvre chante sur le pas de ma porte une langue inconnue et charmante comme une musique fausse*"—"On my doorstep your lips sing an unknown, charming language, like music off-pitch." The singer invites the boy in, but the object of desire moves languidly away.

The *Cinq Mélodies populaires grecques*—"Five Greek Folk Songs"—completed in 1906, are adaptations of actual Greek folk songs, both melodies and lyrics. To these Ravel supplied light-textured accompaniments and harmonic enhancement that are sophisticated but don't encumber the straightforward material. These brief gems are so enjoyable and easy to grasp that overanalysis is a real risk; but they also have moments of piercing, almost mystical beauty, especially the *Chanson de la mariée*—"Bride's Song"—and *Chanson des cueilleuses de lentisques*—"Song of the Lentisk [a plant resin] Gatherers." Ravel uses folklike melodic scales, which have a droning effect, to add color. *Tout gai*—"Be Merry!"—and *Quel galant m'est comparable*—"What Gallant Compares with Me"—are unfussy settings of their lyrics, respectively joyful and proud.

Far from the direct pleasures of the Greek songs, Ravel's next cycle, *Histoires naturelles*—"Natural Histories"—of 1906, is filled with elaborate, often precious verbal and musical conceits. The five songs set wordy poetic descriptions by Jules Renard of four birds: peacock, swan, kingfisher, and guinea fowl, and also a cricket. Ravel's music is pictorial, using music to track the words closely. In the first song, *Le Paon*—"The Peacock"—for example, Ravel depicts the bird's beauty and dignity in a piano accompaniment in a stately rhythm. Later, the singer imitates the bird's loud and pompous mating call. Easily the noblest and most profound, however, is the fourth song, *Le Martin-pêcheur*—"The Kingfisher." The narrator relates his joy at the bird's landing on the end of his fishing rod, mistaking it for a branch, not noticing the human holding it. Ravel paints the solemn joy of the text in sumptuous, Debussy-like harmonies and very slow tempos. The vocal line relates the experience almost conversationally, swelling lyrically in the closing line, beginning "*Et je suis sûr qu'il ne s'est pas envolé de peur*"—"And I'm sure he didn't fly away from fear."

Ravel returns mostly to form with the *Chants populaires*—"Folk Songs"—a pithy cycle four-song cycle of 1910. The broad-minded composer picked texts by regional, sometimes oppressed, minorities to set. They may be heard sung in ordinary French, or to far greater effect, in dialects. That of the Spanish number that opens the set is a bitter reflection by a woman of Galicia in northwest Spain on the wars the local boys ("Gallegos") are drafted to fight by "Castellanos"—people from the dominant province of Castile. Set to a piano line that's one of Ravel's best take-offs on the guitar, her lament ends with a lilting series of "la la"s that for dark irony hold their own against Mahler's songs. The tone of the second song, set in the rarely heard dialect of the rural Limousin region of central France, is sly but light, reminiscent of a medieval *chanson* about shepherds and shepherdesses forgetting their sheep—and themselves. Ironically again, the lilting, innocent sounding music belies the carnality of the text. The third song, set in heavy Roman dialect, is the shortest and least effective of the four. Ravel's gifts were wrong for this ponderous, Puccinian exercise. But the final song, *Chanson hébraïque*, is astonishing. Written mostly in Yiddish with several Hebrew words, the song is in the form a ritualized dialogue between father and son. Folk music has countless examples of this style, but the Scottish ballad "Edward, Edward," and, more recently, Bob Dylan's "A Hard Rain's A-Gonna Fall" may be familiar to you. In those, the repetition of the questions accumulate horror, while in Ravel's song the subject is piety, as the father asks his son Meyer, whom he calls by the affectionate diminutive "Meyerke," five questions about life. Meyerke replies solemnly to each that his sole purpose is to praise God. The music never varies, as the father's lines are sung to a light, dancelike figure and the son's replies are made to plain but impressive chords. Here Ravel's remarkably simple treatment gathers dignity as he carries the difference in tone between father and son through firmly to the end.

From the apparent simplicity of the folk songs, Ravel returns to an absolute complexity with the *Trois Poèmes de Stéphane Mallarmé*. Ravel, like Debussy, admired Mallarmé, a poet of hard-to-translate yet strangely musical verse. Ravel's 1913 settings of these dense, difficult texts show some of his most advanced practice; yet even within the austere textures of the accompaniment and the dissonant harmony, the composer keeps his melodic lines clear. The ensemble accompaniment, consisting of a string quartet, piccolo, flute, clarinet, bass clarinet, and piano is extraordinary and hearing it is one of the pleasures of getting to know this cycle. Despite their difficulty, these are important milestones for Ravel, carefully crafted in his best manner. Don't expect to like them on first hearing, but keep listening.

Dedicated to his colleague and friend Igor Stravinsky, the first song, *Soupir*—"Sigh"—opens with a long introduction of flowing strings and winds, into which the vocal line steals gently. With the second verse ("*Vers l'azur attendri d'Octobre*"—"Toward the softened blue of October") the flowing motion ends, as the accompaniment changes to a more somber one for strings and piano. The singer ends in a low, quiet tone, as the ensemble plays three evaporating recollections of the opening phrases. *Placet futile*—"Futile Petition"—an appeal in sonnet form to "Hébé," cupbearer to the Greek gods, opens with a spiky phrase for the ensemble, but the tone softens once the voice enters. Lyricism increases, finally breaking out into a rich musical phrase with the words "*Nommez-nous*"—"Appoint me." The final song, *Surgi de la croupe et du bond*—"Rising from the Crupper and the Leap"—is the most obscure of the poems, and Ravel gives it the most radical treatment. The melodic line is less regular; the harmony, though rich, is highly dissonant. The metrics are unusually fluid, even for Ravel, and tempos are so slow that they approach motionlessness.

Following the *Chanson hébraïque* of the folk setting, Ravel makes another run at Jewish themes with the *Deux Mélodies hébraïques*—"Two Hebraic Songs"—of 1914. The first piece, *Kaddisch*, captures the immensity of the Kaddish, the majestic prayer for the dead, with a single long-spun, twisting vocal line that resembles what can be heard a synagogue, though purified and perfected, over a quiet instrumental accompaniment that moves at a stately pace alongside. The score has a noble French translation of the prayer that's more frequently performed, but to hear it sung in its native Aramaic—the composer set both languages—is hair-raising. Although it can never be popular, *Kaddisch* is one of Ravel's great works. Next to this titanic conception, its curious, lilting companion, *L'Énigme éternelle*—"The Eternal Question"—seems trivial, though again it makes a stronger impression in Yiddish than French.

Believing the eighteenth-century texts by Évariste Parny to be authentic translations of Madagascan poems, Ravel set three poems as the *Chansons madécasses*—"Madagascan Songs." It later was discovered that Parny neither spoke the language nor visited the island, but wrote them in India, in imitation of a Madagascan poetic form.[1] No matter; the cycle, which Ravel completed in 1926, is a major achievement. As you might expect, exotic influences are strong, and the second song, *Aoua!*, is interesting for its harsh depiction of European colonialists. The first and third songs are respectively erotic and sensuous. To accompany the singer, Ravel chose a singular ensemble consisting of piano, cello, and a flute that doubles on the piccolo in the first and third songs. But the composer makes a great deal of his stripped-down instrumental trio, and the songs sound like nothing else in the repertory.

Knowing a beautifully musical name when he heard one, in *Nahandove*, Ravel takes advantage of the phrase "*Nahandove, ô belle Nahandove*"—"Lovely Nahandove"—that ends every verse in this masterful depiction of desire aroused and fulfilled. A lover sings in the first two verses that the hour for Nahandove's arrival has come, describing the preparation of his bed in an almost abstracted tone. But this changes in the third verse, "*Elle vient*"—"She's coming!"—where, as a breathless Nahandove arrives, the narrator's excitement rises into an unmistakable expression of his desire, then, more sweetly, of arousal and fulfillment. Ravel accomplishes this difficult task tastefully, but there's no mistaking what he's depicting if you follow the text as you listen to the pulsing piano line, the flute changing to the high-pitched piccolo, and the compressing of the cello's line. Postcoital languor is also depicted with rare accuracy and restraint as the singer expresses regret and longing that "*belle Nahandove*" has left; as the song ends he consoles himself with the idea that "*tu reviendras ce soir*"—"you'll return this evening."

A dissonant clang accompanies the war cry *Aoua!* that opens the next song, then the warning "*Méfiez-vous des Blancs, habitants du rivage*"—"Don't trust the white men, inhabitants of the coast." A stalking figure accompanies the angry litany against the settlers who repaid their welcome with forts, "*tonnerre fut renfermé dans des bouches d'airain*"—"thunder in the mouths of brass"—a strange god, and slavery. Ravel has the singer declaim the words almost breathlessly over a continual intensification of the stalking figure. The war cry and warning are sounded again at the climax of the indictment; then, in quick tempo, with the flute imitating a military trumpet, the singer relates how the settlers were wiped out by war, then storms. But the song ends on an iteration of the cry and warning, sullen but inflexible.

The last song, *Il est doux de se coucher*—"How Pleasant It Is to Lie Down"—moves slowly as it captures the feeling of a man lazily watching his women perform their tasks on a hot afternoon. He asks them to dance ("*Que vos pas soient lents*"—"Step slowly") as the piccolo again is called on to express a heightened state, as the singer expresses his critical pleasure at the women's erotic dance. (Apparently it's too hot for sex.) The cello is plucked in striking imitation of a drum. As the evening breeze stirs, the singer lightly orders the women to prepare dinner with the authority of one who's used to being obeyed. Though the quietest of the *Chansons madécasses*, *Il est doux* is no less brilliant than its companion works, as Ravel captures the stillness of the day and sketches its narrator with spare means, in a few vivid strokes.

Don Quichotte à Dulcinée, Ravel's final song cycle and essay in Spanish color, consists of three short but strong songs. Not drawn straight from Cervantes, the lyrics by Paul Morand for a film based on *Don Quixote* depict aspects of the character in a straightforward, folklike manner. In the first, the *Chanson romanesque*—"Romanesque Song"—Quixote makes flamboyant promises to Dulcinea, to the rhythm of a folk song. The second, the *Chanson épique*—"Epic Song"—is a touching and sincere prayer to the angelic warrior saints Michael and George. Here, the combination of an unusual meter and slow tempo give the song a spacious and meditative atmosphere. The third, the charming *Chanson à boire*—"Drinking Song"—is a defiant gesture by Quixote to the joys of wine and his mistress.

Less known but well worth your hearing and acquaintance are the *Trois Chansons pour choeur mixte sans accompagnement*—"Three Songs for Unaccompanied Mixed Chorus." Completed in 1914, these works for a virtuoso choral group are all one could expect from the master's high period. The first, *Nicolette*, tells a Red Riding Hood–like tale in vocal lines that race, then pause, then surge again with masterful metric freedom. Here Ravel looks back with affection at the style of the Renaissance master Clément Jannequin.[2] The second song, *Trois Beaux Oiseaux de paradis*—"Three Lovely Birds of Paradise"—is a lament for France during the hardships of World War I. The three symbolic birds are the red, white, and blue of the French flag. A mournful vocal leap dominates. The cycle closes with another breathless race with a short, brisk *Ronde*—"Round"—a song in which, like "Row, Row, Row Your Boat," entries are made in canonic order. Of course, with its accelerations, slowdowns, and verbal eruptions, this tribute to mythological figures of the forest of course sounds nothing like that plain canon, and it's great fun to hear.

Not all of Ravel's songs belong to cycles; there are individual works that, however, follow the patterns we've seen. A song from 1909 associated with a thumping Greek dance step, the sturdy *Tripatos*, follows Ravel's love of and skill at handling folk material. *Noël des jouets*—"The Toys' Christmas"—of 1905, set to a charming text by the composer, depicts the toys coming to life as the holiday approaches. On a more exalted level, *Les Grands Vents venus d'outremer*—"The Great Winds Coming from Beyond the Sea"—composed in 1906 sets a symbolist poem by Henri de Régnier to an elaborate accompaniment that suits the florid text. *Sur l'Herbe*—"On the Grass"—of 1907 asks for the singer to blend free declamation and rapid changes in tone that move swiftly from serious to playful; Ravel's setting of the poem by Paul Verlaine is brilliant. Two songs from later in the composer's career are also important. *Ronsard à son âme*—"Ronsard to His Soul"—of 1925 sets verses by the sixteenth-century poet Pierre de Ronsard to a floating vocal line over a keyboard accompaniment that continually suggests medieval harmonic practice. Although it recalls the Marot epigrams of twenty-five years earlier, you'll hear how Ravel's lean 1920s style makes the Marot songs sound busy in comparison. The short *Rêves*—"Dreams"—of 1927 sets a somber poem by Léon-Paul Fargue with relatively few notes but more richness and lyricism than the Ronsard song.

10 Listening to Ravel

Considering Ravel's relatively small output, his music, or some of it, at least, is wildly popular. Probably due to its crossover appeal as a light classical work, the *Pavane pour une infante défunte* is represented by a staggering 319 performances on the ArkivMusic website and dozens each on Spotify and the Naxos sites; the *Boléro* presents a similar story. But so does *La Valse*, as serious a work as Ravel wrote, and certainly the grimmest. So the composer clearly speaks to people, and not always in conventionally pleasing ways, and there seem inevitably to be several great recordings of just about everything Ravel wrote.

The two piano soloists on the enclosed CD are noteworthy for several reasons. Vlado Perlemuter (1904–2002), a native of Poland who lived in France, has a direct link to the composer. Perlemuter studied the piano music with Ravel, lending his performances an indirect but convincing authenticity. (Robert Casadesus also worked with the composer, later recording the complete piano music as well; both performances, and many others, are worth hearing.) Perlemuter's light, elegant touch seems ideal for the lacy textures of *Jeux d'eau* and the subtly varying moods of the *Valses nobles et sentimentales*. Martha Argerich is a fire-eating virtuoso, legendary for her speed, accuracy, and temperament. She's also a great Ravel player, though more fiery than Perlemuter (or Casadesus, for that matter). She makes the G Major concerto's opening movement as brilliant and impressive as it can be. If you find that you love this work, you'll also need to listen to Arturo Benedetti Michelangeli's version.

The poise of the Kodály Quartet's recording of the String Quartet brings out the manifold beauties of the second movement, etching its Javanese influences with charm and a light touch. The first movement of the Piano Trio gets deluxe treatment in a plush performance by the Arden Trio, which holds its own amid stiff competition. Like so much of the master's oeuvre, this great work is represented by several performances some of us can't live without, including that of the Beaux Arts Trio and a profoundly poetic rendition by the Soviet-era Oistrakh Trio. And in the realm of ultimate luxury, there's a 1950 performance by three legendary players: violinist Jascha Heifetz, pianist Arthur Rubinstein, and cellist Gregor Piatigorsky.

Michael Gielen's light, cool touch is well suited to part 3 of *Daphnis et Chloé* with the South West German Radio Symphony Orchestra, as every note comes through clearly. Another authoritative performance of the complete ballet is that of the Boston Symphony Orchestra under Charles Munch. And finally, the American soprano Arleen Auger is marvelous in *Asie*, the first song from the *Shéhérazade* cycle, yet another selection where the competition is heavy. The bright, sweet timbre of Auger's voice is distinctive, and her interpretation blends passion with high intelligence and absolute clarity of diction. Other recordings of *Shéhérazade* you'll want to hear feature Victoria de los Angeles and Régine Crespin.

I was hoping to include an excerpt from *L'Enfant et les sortilèges*, but there simply wasn't room. Presumably this taste of several high points of Ravel's output will stimulate your appetite for more. In assembling this CD I kept thinking in terms of taking cream from the top, but with Ravel, almost everything falls into that category.

Notes

Chapter 2: His Life

1. Roger Nichols, *Ravel*, p. 353.
2. Ibid., pp. 51–53.
3. Ibid., p. 104.
4. Benjamin Ivry, *Maurice Ravel: A Life*, p. 41.
5. Donald Francis Tovey, *Chamber Music*, p. 19.
6. Arbie Orenstein, *Ravel, Man and Musician*, pp. 77–78.
7. Nichols, p. 207.
8. Orenstein, p. 108.
9. Oliver Sacks, *Musicophilia*, p. 348.
10. Nichols, p. 347

Chapter 3: The Piano Music

1. Paul Roberts, *Reflections: The Piano Music of Maurice Ravel*, p. 41.
2. Quoted in Roberts, pp. 126–127.
3. See Roberts, pp. 37–47.
4. Nichols, p. 75.
5. Roy Howat, *The Art of French Piano Music*, pp. 183–186.
6. Roberts, pp. 75–84.
7. Nichols, p. 103.
8. See Howat, pp. 145–158.

Chapter 5: The Concertos

1. Laurence Davies, *Ravel Orchestral Music*, pp. 46–47.
2. Orenstein, p. 205.
3. See Davies, p. 47.

Chapter 6: The Chamber Music

1. Orenstein, p. 162.
2. See Orenstein, pp. 144–145.

Chapter 7: The Orchestral Works

1. Ivry, p. 50.
2. Orenstein, pp. 69–70.
3. Ivry, pp. 132–133.
4. Quoted in Ivry, p. 73.
5. David Hurwitz, *The Mahler Symphonies: An Owner's Manual*, pp. 15–17.
6. Orenstein, p. 119.
7. Davies, p. 30.
8. Joseph Campbell, *The Hero with a Thousand Faces*, p. 81.
9. Quoted in Ivry, p. 76.
10. Nichols, pp. 304–305.
11. Ivry, p. 116.
12. See Hurwitz, p. 192.
13. Quoted in Orenstein, pp. 200–201.
14. Ivry, p. 157.
15. Ibid., p. 158.

Chapter 8: The Operas

1. Liner notes to *L'Heure espagnole*, INA Mémoire Vive, CD IMV027.
2. Ivry, pp. 130–132.

Chapter 9: The Works for Voice

1. Orenstein, p. 194.
2. Ibid., p. 184.

Selected Bibliography

Bertrand, Aloysius. *Gaspard de la nuit.* Translated by Donald Sidney-Fryer. Encino, CA: Black Coat Press, 2004.

Campbell, Joseph. *The Hero with a Thousand Faces.* New York: MJF Books, 1949.

Davies, Laurence. *Ravel Orchestral Music.* BBC Music Guides. Seattle: University of Washington Press, 1971.

Friskin, James, and Irwin Freundlich. *Music for the Piano.* New York: Dover Publications, 1975.

Guinn, John, and Les Stone, eds. *The St. James Opera Encyclopedia.* Detroit: Visible Ink Press, 1997.

Howat, Roy. *The Art of French Piano Music.* New Haven, CT: Yale University Press, 2009.

Hurwitz, David. *The Mahler Symphonies: An Owner's Manual.* Pompton Plains, NJ: Amadeus Press, 2004.

Ivry, Benjamin. *Maurice Ravel: A Life.* New York: Welcome Rain, 2000.

Jankélévitch, Vladimir. *Ravel.* Reprint, Westport, CT: Greenwood Press, 1976.

Kennedy, Michael, ed. *The Oxford Dictionary of Music.* 2nd ed. Oxford: Oxford University Press, 1994.

Nichols, Roger. *Ravel.* New Haven, CT: Yale University Press, 2011.

Orenstein, Arbie. *Ravel, Man and Musician.* New York: Dover Publications, 1991.

Ravel, Maurice. *Boléro.* Pocket score. Paris: Editions Durand, n.d.

———. *Chansons madécasses*. Paris: Editions Durand, n.d.

———. *Concerto pour la main gauche*. Paris: Editions Durand, 1931.

———. *Concerto pour piano et orchestre*. Paris: Editions Durand, 1932.

———. *Daphnis et Chloé*. Full score. Mineola, NY: Dover Publications, 1989.

———. *Daphnis et Chloé, Suites 1 and 2*. Full score. Mineola, NY: Dover Publications, 2006.

———. *Introduction and Allegro for Harp, with String Quartet, Flute and Clarinet*. Pocket score. New York: International Music Co., n.d.

———. *La Valse*. Pocket score. Mineola, NY: Dover Publications, 2004.

———. *L'Enfant et les sortilèges*. Full score. Paris: Editions Durand, n.d.

———. *L'Enfant et les sortilèges*. Vocal score. Paris: Editions Durand, n.d.

———. *"Le Tombeau de Couperin" and Other Works for Solo Piano*. Mineola, NY: Dover Publications, 1997.

———. *L'Heure espagnole*. Full score. Paris: Editions Durand, n.d.

———. *L'Heure espagnole*. Vocal score. Paris: Editions Durand, n.d.

———. *Ma Mère L'Oye*. Full score of ballet version. New York: Edwin F. Kalmus, 1988.

———. *Piano Masterpieces of Maurice Ravel*. New York: Dover Publications, 1986.

———. *Sonate pour violon et piano*. Paris: Editions Durand, n.d.

———. *Songs, 1896–1914*. Arbie Orenstein, ed. New York: Dover, 1990.

Roberts, Paul, *Reflections: The Piano Music of Maurice Ravel.* Montclair, NJ: Amadeus Press, 2012.

Roland-Manuel. *Maurice Ravel.* Translated by Cynthia Jolly. New York: Dover Publications, 1972.

Sacks, Oliver. *Musicophilia.* Revised and expanded edition. New York: Vintage Books, 2008.

Said, Edward W. *Culture and Imperialism.* New York: Vintage Books, 1994.

———. *Orientalism.* New York: Vintage Books, 1979.

Tovey, Donald Francis. *Chamber Music.* Oxford: Oxford University Press, 1989.

CD Track Listing

1. *Jeux d'eau* (5:32)

   Vlado Perlemuter, piano
   From Nimbus CD NI7713-14

2. *Valses nobles et sentimentales* (14:07)

   Vlado Perlemuter, piano
   From Nimbus CD NI7713-14

3. Piano Concerto in G Major: Allegramente (first movement) (8:20)

   Martha Argerich, piano; Gary Bertini, conductor, Cologne Radio Symphony Orchestra
   From Capriccio CD C71093

4. String Quartet in F Major: *Assez vif. Très rythmé* (second movement) (6:14)

   Kodály Quartet
   From Naxos CD 8.550249

5. Trio in A Minor: *Modéré* (first movement) (8:59)

   Arden Trio
   From Delos CD DE3055

6. *Daphnis et Chloé*, Part 3: *Lever du jour* (6:03)

   Michael Gielen, conductor, South West German Radio Symphony Orchestra and the Europe Choir Academy
   From SWR Klassik CD CD93.197

7. *Daphnis et Chloé*, Part 3: *Pantomime* (6:47)

   Michael Gielen, conductor, South West German Radio Symphony Orchestra and the Europe Choir Academy
   From SWR Klassik CD CD93.197

8. *Daphnis et Chloé*, Part 3: *Danse générale* (*Bacchanale*) (4:29)

   Michael Gielen, conductor, South West German Radio Symphony Orchestra and the Europe Choir Academy
   From SWR Klassik CD CD93.197

9. *Asie*, from *Shéhérazade* (10:16)

   Arleen Auger, soprano; Ernest Bour, conductor, South West German Radio Symphony Orchestra
   From SWR Klassik CD CD93.111

Musical recordings under license from Naxos of America, www.Naxos.com.

UNLOCKING THE MASTERS

The highly acclaimed Unlocking the Masters series brings readers into the world of the greatest composers and their music. All books come with CDs that have tracks taken from the world's foremost libraries of recorded classics, bringing the music to life.

"With infectious enthusiasm and keen insight, the Unlocking the Masters series succeeds in opening our eyes, ears, hearts, and minds to the great composers." – *Strings*

H'S CHORAL MUSIC:
STENER'S GUIDE
Gordon Jones
.99 • 978-1-57467-180-3
0332767

CH'S KEYBOARD MUSIC:
STENER'S GUIDE
Victor Lederer
2.99 • 978-1-57467-182-7
00332830

THOVEN'S CHAMBER MUSIC:
ISTENER'S GUIDE
Victor Lederer
2.99 • 978-1-57467-203-9
00333394

ETHOVEN'S PIANO MUSIC:
LISTENER'S GUIDE
Victor Lederer
2.99 • 978-1-57467-194-0
00333060

ETHOVEN'S SYMPHONIES:
GUIDED TOUR
John Bell Young
22.99 • 978-1-57467-169-8
L00331951

ERNSTEIN'S ORCHESTRAL MUSIC:
N OWNER'S MANUAL
y David Hurwitz
24.99 • 978-1-57467-193-3
L00332912

HOPIN: A LISTENER'S GUIDE
O THE MASTER OF THE PIANO
y Victor Lederer
22.99 • 978-1-57467-148-3
00331699

EXPLORING HAYDN:
A LISTENER'S GUIDE TO
MUSIC'S BOLDEST INNOVATOR
by David Hurwitz
$29.99 • 978-1-57467-116-2
HL00331671

LISZT: A LISTENER'S GUIDE
by John Bell Young
$22.99 • 978-1-57467-170-4
HL00331952

THE MAHLER SYMPHONIES:
AN OWNER'S MANUAL
by David Hurwitz
$22.99 • 978-1-57467-099-8
HL00331650

OPERA'S FIRST MASTER:
THE MUSICAL DRAMAS OF
CLAUDIO MONTEVERDI
by Mark Ringer
$29.95 • 978-1-57467-110-0
HL00331665

GETTING THE MOST OUT OF
MOZART: THE VOCAL WORKS
by David Hurwitz
$22.95 • 978-1-57467-106-3
HL00331661

RAVEL: A LISTENER'S GUIDE
by Victor Lederer
$19.99 • 978-1-57467-477-4
HL00139970

SCHUBERT: A SURVEY OF HIS
SYMPHONIC, PIANO, AND
CHAMBER MUSIC
by John Bell Young
$22.99 • 978-1-57467-177-3
HL00332766

SCHUBERT'S THEATER OF SONG:
A LISTENER'S GUIDE
by Mark Ringer
$22.99 • 978-1-57467-176-6
HL00331973

SHOSTAKOVICH SYMPHONIES
AND CONCERTOS:
AN OWNER'S MANUAL
by David Hurwitz
$24.99 • 978-1-57467-131-5
HL00331692

SIBELIUS, THE ORCHESTRAL
WORKS: AN OWNER'S MANUAL
by David Hurwitz
$27.95 • 978-1-57467-149-0
HL00331735

RICHARD STRAUSS:
AN OWNER'S MANUAL
by David Hurwitz
$24.99 • 978-1-57467-442-2
HL00119744

VERDI: THE OPERAS AND
CHORAL WORKS
by Victor Lederer
$24.99 • 978-1-57467-440-8
HL00118902

DECODING WAGNER:
AN INVITATION TO HIS WORLD
OF MUSIC DRAMA
by Thomas May
$27.99 • 978-1-57467-097-4
HL00331649

AMADEUS
PRESS
www.amadeuspress.com
Prices and availability subject
to change without notice.

0815